HELLSGRIN

Center Point
Large Print

Also by Steve Frazee and available from
Center Point Large Print:

Fire in the Valley
Four Graves West
Look Behind Every Hill

**This Large Print Book carries the
Seal of Approval of N.A.V.H.**

HELLSGRIN

STEVE FRAZEE

CENTER POINT LARGE PRINT
THORNDIKE, MAINE

This Center Point Large Print edition
is published in the year 2019 by arrangement with
Golden West Literary Agency.

Originally published in the US by Rinehart
Originally published in the UK by Bruce & Watson

The text of this Large Print edition is unabridged.
In other aspects, this book may vary
from the original edition.
Printed in the United States of America
on permanent paper.
Set in 16-point Times New Roman type.

ISBN: 978-1-64358-236-8 (hardcover)
ISBN: 978-1-64358-240-5 (paperback)

Library of Congress Cataloging-in-Publication Data

Names: Frazee, Steve, 1909-1992, author.
Title: Hellsgrin / Steve Frazee.
Description: Large Print edition. | Thorndike, Maine :
    Center Point Large Print, 2019.
Identifiers: LCCN 2019013349| ISBN 9781643582368 (hardcover :
    alk. paper) | ISBN 9781643582405 (pbk. : alk. paper)
Subjects: LCSH: Large type books. | GSAFD: Western stories.
Classification: LCC PS3556.R358 H45 2019 | DDC 813/.54—dc23
LC record available at https://lccn.loc.gov/2019013349

HELLSGRIN

ONE

By late afternoon no one had come. Johnny Bennion was a week early himself, but every hour that passed and left the basin below him still deserted was that much more time that he could continue to nurse the wild hope that he was the only one who remembered.

He worked slowly, repairing the drift fence smashed by a snowslide the winter before. From where he was, about a quarter of a mile below the glacier, he could see every trail but one that led to the long-dead town of Basin City.

The one route that Bennion could not see was the Hellsgrin Trail, off to his left. It came up from the basin with lung-searing steepness, then crawled through the rocks above the great bergschrund, the arcing crevasse at the head of the glacier, and from there it rose almost to 13,000 feet before crossing the Granite Range.

Lonely cairns still marked the Hellsgrin Trail. Bennion had seen them. But that trail was for burros or mules handled by men with steel in their guts; he was not worried about anyone's coming in that way.

He dug postholes in the bouldery glacial debris. He went downhill to retrieve wire from the wrecked fence. A lean and wiry man in his early thirties, Bennion was used to the altitude, but he did not hurry. Now and then he stopped to scan the willow flats along the twisting run of the Sorrowful River below the town.

The very head of the Sorrowful was only a few feet away, an icy gush that came from under Hellsgrin Glacier. It pitched down the mountain in white cascades, then leveled off where it struck the silt-laden dams at the Yankee Blade and Golden Hoof mills near the town. Below that the beavers had the stream in check for two miles, and then it disappeared into the canyon.

The only wagon road into Basin City had come up the canyon only a few feet above the water. Year after year spring floods had washed out sections of it, until cursing mineowners had sworn they would build a new road over the Flying Horse Mountains.

Economics would have forced the mining companies to a new road location in time, for their investors howled louder each year about the terrible cost of rebuilding the canyon passage; but Basin City did not last long enough to have a new road. It was a late camp, founded in 1902. It began to sag when the pockety deposits of the Midas, the Golden Hoof, the Emancipator and other smaller mines were exhausted after five years.

It collapsed when the big mine, the Yankee Blade, with its incredibly rich golden chimney of ore, shut down in the winter of 1909. Diehards hung on after that, leasing, pecking away, packing in supplies over the long, difficult trails. By 1912 Basin City was almost abandoned.

Prospectors for a time continued to make the town their summer headquarters, always hopeful of discovering something that five thousand men before them had been too blind to see. And then the old-time prospectors, the genuine infantry patrols of mining history, who covered the ground the hard way, began to disappear. They died, they wandered into oblivion on disappearing frontiers. A few of them settled on the crowded edges of civilization, full of tales that no one cared to hear.

Basin City was a ghost town by 1914, so remote and hard to reach that years passed when no man went to it. Then after a second world war the new prospector came. He was airborne, probing from on high with instruments far removed from pick and shovel. His light, slow planes passed over Basin City and skimmed the mountains all around it, but nothing came back to send him to the ground with heavy machinery to build roads.

The planes went on to other mountains and the shell of the town stayed as it had been for more than half a century. No jeep could reach the basin; the pack trails were sliding in or growing dim with grass. Few men knew, or cared, where the ghost town was, and even fewer had any reason to go near it.

And yet Bennion knew that this was the month when They would appear. One week from today would be the twelfth of September, fifty years and one hundred and sixty-four days since Alonzo Pike started up the Hellsgrin Trail the last time.

Bennion watched the road below town. It was a faint, broken line that dipped in and out of beaver-flooded ground beside the willows. Anyone coming off Volcano Pass would strike the road. Anyone braving the canyon route would have to appear on the same road.

Like the trail around Hellsgrin Glacier, the route by which Bennion had come was not a likely one for strangers. His ranch twenty miles away across the Granite Mountains was astride the entrance to the trail.

That in itself was a deterrent to casual travel, and then the trail beyond the ranch was branching, vague in many places, most difficult to follow.

Thirty miles west, below the Sorrowful Canyon, Sandy Mulford ran a dude ranch near where the old road from Basin City reached level ground. He never sent pack trips into the canyon, for that meant swimming and fording the river in seventeen places where the road was washed away. Bennion knew; he had counted them.

As low as the river was now, an experienced man could take horses through the canyon without too great risk to himself and the animals. It was not the best route, but still it was the sure one for a stranger to the area because he could not get lost after he was in the canyon.

That was the most likely route by which they would come. They? That was the vagueness which troubled Bennion, the question he could not answer. *They* could be anyone who knew what Stony Jackson, the Yankee Blade engineer, had predicted fifty years before.

Bennion did not like the pronoun; its use belonged to someone with an unbalanced mind, someone who lumped all fears and enemies, real and fancied, under the term *they.* But it was the only word he could use.

A cold wind from Hellsgrin chilled the sweat along the edges of his short black hair. Without looking behind him he still saw the glacier, knew what it was, for he had lived a long time with it as a disturbing part of his thinking.

He rested, looking at the two ranges that held the basin in a mighty grip. On his right, the Flying Horses, dark timbered, jumbled. The harsh gray Granite Range surged in on the left, deep scored with channels that ran almost to the creek near town. It seemed that the two ranges had raced to encircle the basin and had collided with an awful impact when they reached the head of it where Hellsgrin Glacier was.

There the Flying Horses ended. The Granites

11

ran on to the east and then swung north, ragged, broken but still impassable unless one knew the crossings.

Bennion's horses, Frog and Stranger, gave him the first warning. They stopped foraging on the boulder-strewn slope and stood with their ears cocked forward, looking at something in the basin.

Reflection from the falling sun made a golden liveness in the windows of the town. The new tin roof on the Nose Paint Saloon threw a blaze in Bennion's eyes until he laid his hammer on top of a post and shaded his vision with both hands.

He studied intently the broken course of the road below town. Nothing was moving down there. After a time the horses returned to their eating, but now and then they raised their heads to look below. Bennion knew from their behavior that they saw something, something familiar, and classified as harmless. Horses?

Bennion's pack and his saddle were on the ground. He went to the saddle and uncased his binoculars. The ponds below town came into sharp focus. He saw a beaver ripple close to a dam and the smoky grayness of water-killed spruce trees standing in the water. He moved over to the road and scanned the broken links until vision grew blurry where the Sorrowful began its canyon run.

For five long minutes he studied the country.

Nothing. But he did not quit; there was something down there. Movement had caught the eyes of the horses. Bennion had to know what it was. Without the glasses he tried the trick of looking with the more perceptive outer edges of his vision.

When he saw the movement it was quite clear. A cow elk and her calf moved out of the willows, then disappeared again at the edge of a pond. They were leisurely, unalarmed. The horses saw them and went back to eating.

Bennion put the glasses away. He stood quietly, frowning at the tenseness that was slowly leaving him. He was an easy-going man and knew it. Air Force doctors had told him he had a slow heart, but now he could hear it beating. Was that a measure of how bad this thing was going to be, or merely excitement he had built up in his own mind?

He estimated his unfinished work. To close the gap again he needed eight new posts. Timbers from the Yankee Blade mill would do. The wire he needed was stored in the saloon. As he gathered up his tools he felt a vague reluctance about going on down to Basin City. The feeling stayed with him as he put the pack on Frog and saddled Stranger.

He followed the switchback trail beside the plunging stream that came from Hellsgrin. After he had gone two hundred yards, he stopped to look back at the glacier. The great mass of ice and snow twisted down from between black rock fangs. A cliff, or hanging glacier, it was, sternly held in the crush of the granite.

No longer was there snow and cold enough for Hellsgrin to have a valley glacier. In ancient times, according to Stony Jackson, Hellsgrin had extended at least thirty-five miles. It had gouged the great basin where the town was, grinding, moving, alive with a slowness that was time itself.

Its blue-white power had crumbled granite and in its icy grip it had carried rocks that weighed ten thousand tons. Like a ball mill, the glacier had rolled and ground those stones to exceeding smoothness, leaving some of still monstrous size below Sandy Mulford's Bonnet B on the Sorrowful.

A very small glacier, Jackson said. It was much smaller now, about two miles long, but it was still defying time, and maybe it was sneering at Jackson's estimate of it. Because of Jackson and his studies of the glacier, Bennion was here today, worrying about others who were coming.

He felt a sudden irritation over Jackson's work and smug pronouncement. Who was he to hold a stopwatch on Hellsgrin? Sure, he had been a fine mining engineer, and his monograph on Hellsgrin was the only one existing, but . . .

Bennion had studied everything he could find

14

about Stony Jackson, including stories about him in newspapers, most of which existed now only as files in dusty morgues.

Jackson had been a man given to bluntness. His reports were categorical. "Further exploration of the Midas claims would be a waste of time and money." *The Argonaut* said, "Stony Jackson, the well known mining engineer, is in our city after a week of touring the new excitement on the Duck Foot. He says the boys won't find enough gold there in one hundred years to buy two drinks of poor whiskey."

That was Jackson. Time had borne out the truth of most of his statements about mining, and in spite of his present irritation, Bennion felt that he would have liked the man, having formed what he considered an accurate picture of him as an individual. But was that enough?

Gruff and professionally incorruptible and competent in an era that preferred incompetence in his field, was Morton Stonewall Jackson, but what did he know of glaciers? In spite of his mathematical skill and confidence and all the time he had devoted to Hellsgrin, the thought persisted that he must be considered an amateur concerning glaciers.

Yet, with a bluntness that he had scarcely applied to mining reports, Jackson had predicted the movement of Hellsgrin to the hour, minute and second.

September 12, 1959, at 2:19 P.M.

At that time the body of Alonzo Pike would be at a line between two steel drills set in the rocks, one and five-eighths miles from where he had gone into a crevasse.

Bennion doubted the prediction; but he was here because he also believed it.

Hellsgrin stared down at him. The falling sun was on the plunging icefall that was the end of the glacier, but it put no soft tints or beauty on the grim tumble of ice.

I am time far beyond your knowing, the glacier said. *Let men argue about glacial periods or one great glacial era. I was here then. I am here now, dying, but I will stay for centuries to come.*

Hellsgrin was right. A forgotten Mountain Man had named it. He must have seen it from high above, a two-mile streak of choppy teeth set between ragged gums of black rock.

Bennion led the horses down the mountain, and he felt that he was going deeper into ice that once had covered all the basin.

Now the strike of sun was gone from the roof of the Nose Paint Saloon. The windows of the town were dead and Basin City appeared as it really was, loneliness left by the sweep of time.

The sound impression came through slowly above the splashing of the glacier stream. It was a plane, of course. The big liners and the streaking jets often flew directly over the basin. Helicopter? Bennion thought of that when the sound persisted and nothing showed against the sky.

It could be done. It would take a powerful one, though, to rise from the basin after landing. He led his horses away from the plunging stream until he could hear without interference. The voice of civilization is an engine. He was right, he was hearing an engine, but it was not in a plane.

Suddenly Bennion was a man caught short on his own ground. He was hearing the high-pitched engine of a jeep somewhere on this side of the Flying Horses. It could not be! There was no way to get a jeep across those mountains.

Until he actually saw the vehicle, he still argued against a fact accomplished. His glasses picked it up when it came to the head of a long frontal slope, clear of the timber. My God! The fool was not going to go down that slope! It was soft ground, full of buried boulders.

Going straight, the driver might make it, but he could not keep the jeep headed straight down all the way because there was a cliff which apparently the man could not see from where he was. He would see it, all right, when he had to turn and angle along the steep soft slope to go around it, and that was when he would be in big trouble. The jeep would crab downhill when he turned. Ten to one it would roll and if it did, it would go all the way to the bottom.

The man was a maniac for sure if he tried that descent. Ah, he was not going to try! He began to lurch back and forth in short movements to get his wheels cut around. The engine gave full-throated outcry as he dug uphill.

Still angled a little against the downslope, the jeep slewed. It lurched and almost tipped and then it settled in and clawed uphill, disappearing into the timber, but it did not go far because the engine was silent a moment later.

Bennion lowered the glasses and shook his head. How in the name of Tophet had that man ever got across the Flying Horses? The other side, particularly, was a wild and rugged wilderness where even horses found hard going.

But he was here, not two miles away. Now he would leave the jeep and come in on foot.

Then Bennion heard the engine start again. He swung the binoculars up. Hellsfire! The driver had not quit; he had merely turned to get a straight shot at the descent and now he was moving again. He was backing down!

Bennion could not see the winchline, but that must be it. The man had anchored it to a tree when he pulled uphill. Winch or not, he was still headed for suicide because he was backing in a dead line toward the cliff.

Bennion wanted to cry out across the distance, "Hold it! Hold it!"

The jeep kept moving in a series of bumps and jerks. Then apparently something slipped and the vehicle was out of control, rushing toward the cliff. Bennion thought it was gone. It slowed, yawing on the end of the line. It rocked as the front wheels caught in the soft slope and turned at a dangerous angle. When it came to a slamming stop short of the cliff edge, Bennion let his breath out.

He saw the driver get out. In the failing light there was little to tell about him except that he took the prize for idiocy. It was one thing to have guts and another to have a little judgment. This man was way short on judgment or he would not have tackled the Flying Horses in the first place.

Just one man? That was all Bennion could see. The fellow seemed to be getting back into the jeep. No, he was fooling around on the wrong side. A few minutes later he started down the hill on foot.

In relief Bennion let out a fervent oath.

So absorbed had he been in rooting for the man's safety he had forgotten for a moment that the fellow was the first of the Theys, the unknown adversaries. Once more he scanned the road and then he went on down the mountain.

Not counting ruined mine buildings across the creek, forty structures of various kinds were still standing in Basin City. Those in soft earth near the stream were tilted at drunken angles, but on the rocky ground along the main street there were still some solid buildings.

Bennion had wrecked several buildings to get lumber to repair some of the more substantial ones, so that now there were four comfortably inhabitable places, including the barroom of the Nose Paint. The rest of the saloon he had left to fall apart, but he had done considerable work on the barroom and the log storeroom attached to it.

He generally stayed in the Nose Paint on his trips to Basin City, except at times when the history of the town worked an unease in him, and then he preferred to camp outside among the ancient wagons in the Poor Boy freight yard.

That evening was one of the times when he chose to stay outside.

When he turned the horses loose, they shook and dipped their heads and trotted off toward the creek. Let them be the first evidence to the man coming up the road that he was not alone in Basin City.

Surrounded by the hulks of giant ore wagons, Bennion made his camp and began to cook his supper. Old Lucius Morgan had run the Poor Boy freighting outfit in the booming days of Basin City, charging fat per-pound prices for everything he hauled up the canyon road.

When he heard the rumor that the Yankee Blade

and the other big mines were going to close for good, he made a fast deal and sold out to a saloonman thirty miles away at Smelter Town. A month later the mines shut down. The road washed out in the canyon not long afterward, leaving the new owner with most of his rolling stock trapped in a dead camp.

The saloonman weighed the cost of rebuilding the road against the value of the wagons—and left them where they were. Now grass was growing under them and time had combed deep furrows in the heavy oaken wheels and tongues.

The wagons stood like everything else around Bennion, things too sturdy to die but lost and hopelessly waiting out time.

And Bennion thought, A hell of a mood I'm in this evening.

When the sun was bright on Basin City, and Bennion was busy working out his plans for the place, then the ghosts of long ago seldom troubled him. He could picture them from the facts he had learned about them through hard research, and they were only men who had raised their voices here and then gone on to stillness. Now they troubled him; there was too much he did not know about them.

And Stony Jackson's date was close, so close that someone else besides Johnny Bennion was proving himself a believer.

He heard the man when he came off the sod

and struck the crunchy gravel of the street. He must have seen the horses. He surely had seen the smoke of Bennion's fire. Let him come to Bennion. But he did not come, this first of the Theys.

An old board cracked under weight. The fellow was looking into buildings as he went. He opened and closed some of the doors of the structures Bennion had repaired. When he went into the saloon, Bennion recognized the scraping noise the door made against the floor.

That door did not close, and after a time Bennion saw the first streak of smoke come out of the stovepipe. That was the most comfortable place, all right, stocked with food, with wood cut and stacked along the wall, with bunks, and with the best of the furniture Bennion had salvaged from the town.

Even an idiot who had been forced to leave his jeep hanging on the mountainside could see the advantages of the Nose Paint Saloon.

Bennion poured himself another cup of coffee. Let the other man wait and stew and wonder about his competition. Who he was was not at all important. What he was—there was the problem.

The visitor did not come until just before dusk.

TWO

Bennion heard him on the saloon porch, and then the gravelly sound as he crossed the street, and then the footsteps were soft on the grass that edged out from the freight-yard fence. Fabric made a sharp tearing noise when the man scrambled through the sagging fence on the street side of the yard.

Bennion rose to meet the visitor. It was a woman.

She was tall, with short dark hair, dressed in jeans and a gray wool shirt. About twenty-five, Bennion guessed.

"I'm Gail McBride."

They stared at each other in silence. A good looking, well-designed chick and no mistake, Bennion thought. Her expression was cool and intent as she drew her own opinion of him. She gave him the impression that she was thinking fast and accurately, without any strain; but all at once she started to take a cigarette from her shirt pocket and then at the last moment took her hand away with a quick, deliberate movement, as if rebuking an unconscious reaction.

Bennion offered her a cigarette. She shook her head. He said, "Which way did you—No! Not the green jeep up there on the cliff?"

"It's not on the cliff. I can get out of there."

"How'd you get that thing over the mountains?"

She answered with her mind on something else. "There's a road to the top."

For the second time Bennion resented being caught short on his own ground. "What road?" There had been no road to the top of the Flying Horses a month before.

"To some mining claims. The bulldozers are still working on it down in the timber."

Bennion grunted his distaste. "Uranium promoters."

"This happens to be aquamarine. They've got it, too."

She talked as if she knew something about mining.

"I told you my name," she said.

"Yeah, you did." And it meant nothing. Bennion glanced toward his fire. "Coffee?"

"No thank you." She waited.

"I'm John Bennion."

"Oh! Johnny Bennion."

Now it was his turn to wait. "So?" he asked.

"I heard about you in Randall. They said you wouldn't let anyone through your ranch."

"Some people, no."

She was more at ease, as if she had found Bennion not as formidable as expected. She lit a cigarette with casual sureness, her glance taking in his camp, the firesite, the cooking gear

24

on an overturned wagon box, his tools lying on the spokes of a wheel cast aside and now laced through with weeds.

"I saw you working on your fence," she said.

That must have been before he saw her, Bennion thought, because she had been too busy on that slope to do any looking around after he spotted her. She must have stopped in the timber before he heard the jeep.

"I was merely studying out the country ahead," she said.

"Sure."

Suddenly they were both looking toward Hellsgrin. In the dusk the glacier hung white, grim, massive on the plunging face of the mountain. It was a mighty waterfall congealed in the rocks, poised to come roaring down. Silent, ageless, Hellsgrin was there.

When they turned to each other again, the woman's quiet, waiting expression told Bennion there was no doubt that the glacier had brought her to Basin City. She knew who he was, beyond his name, so there was nothing for her to wonder about concerning his reasons for being here. At least, if he explained a little, she ought to understand.

It was a time to talk. They ought to get together, put their interests and their problems before each other openly, come to an agreement, an alliance, before others reached Basin City. In

Gail McBride's dark eyes Bennion thought he saw the same reasoning. She seemed uncertain, seemed to be weighing a course of action.

"You know that I'm Alonzo Pike's grandson," Bennion said.

"Yes." She hesitated. "I know that much about you."

"All right then, that puts you completely ahead of me." She did not answer, so Bennion said, "Who are you?"

She had changed before he asked the flat question. She was wary. "I'm Gail McBride," she said, and that was a rejection of his attempt to put things in the open.

Bennion sat down on the wagon box. He had made his offer and now he was not going to try to change her refusal by arguing. If no one else showed up, they would probably come around to an understanding.

"You *were* alone in that jeep, weren't you?" Bennion asked.

"Yes."

"Want any help getting it the rest of the way down?"

"I think I can make it."

"Fine!" Bennion lit a cigarette. "Watch the door on the saloon, will you? It closes hard. If a rat gets inside . . ."

"I'll be careful about that."

Darkness was close. Burning steadily on oak

26

from a wrecked wagon, the fire was rapidly becoming the focal point of their attention between words. Soon it would overpower the view of the ghostly wagons, the buildings, even the mountains and the fading whiteness of Hellsgrin.

The woman had not moved from where she stopped when she walked up. Between glances at the fire, she kept watching Bennion. "You own Basin City now, don't you?"

Bennion nodded. He had bought a tax certificate on the townsite five years before, and on the placer claims below town, and on millsites along the base of the Flying Horses. In fact, almost the entire basin was his. He figured about two miles of fence placed in the right places would close things off on the west and north.

The mountains themselves on the south, with the Hellsgrin Trail blocked, would hold that side of the basin, and his drift fence below the glacier already controlled exit to the east. The grass would support fifty head of cows during the short high-country summer.

"And you bought the Yankee Blade Number One," Gail McBride said. "What does that entitle you to?"

"To the whole fifteen hundred feet." Collapsed portal with gray timbers sticking out of the muck, a caved tunnel, and a glory hole that had been a stope in the great funnel of gold ore. In 1902 the owners of the Yankee Blade had refused the offer of an English syndicate to buy the mine for three million, cash. Assessed valuation in 1946, when Bennion made his bid, two hundred dollars. He had bought it for half the assessed valuation plus advertising costs.

"You know the history of the Yankee Blade?" Bennion asked.

"Some of it."

That was an honest answer. *Some of it.* The rest of it was buried in the hard ice of Hellsgrin Glacier.

"What did you want with the mine?" the woman asked.

"I wanted the five hundred by six hundred feet of it that runs out into the basin. The rest I'll sell you, or anyone else, for two bits."

"I'm not interested." Gail McBride turned away. Firelight showed the triangular rip she had torn in the seat of her jeans coming through the fence. "Good night, Mr. Bennion."

"Go to the left. You can squeeze between the fence and the building without ripping your pants."

She walked into the darkness unhurriedly. Bennion heard her cross the street, and then the door of the Nose Paint scraped open, and closed solidly.

She was scared, Bennion thought. In spite of her poise, she had been good and scared all the time she was talking to him, and that was the reason she had been so sparing with her answers and so curt with her questions.

I'm scared too, Bennion thought, and it was the same kind of fear he remembered from all the final runs he had made over targets in a B-29, those leveling-out moments when you had to hold the course and take the flak and depend on others to beat off the screaming fighters that came in.

The hell with saying you got used to those moments of waiting, or ever thought you were the one they could not touch. There was the edge of that old uneasiness in him now, with no one to back him up and a much longer wait ahead.

He built up the fire and sat down on his rolled sleeping bag. So long ago, the things that had happened here. The long silence was on Basin City. The place deserved forgetting, but that was impossible.

Fifty years was a monstrous period for any question to hang suspended in time.

They came as they had come before on lonely nights when Bennion lay just before sleeping in the Nose Paint, where their boot sounds and their laughter and their curses once had rocked the walls. They came from the mesmerism of the fire, from the almighty silence of the basin, the ghosts of those who had walked here young and strong, like lords.

There was Peyton R. Shores, the dandy whose sartorial elegance was always mentioned in the newspapers wherever he went. He was the general manager of the Yankee Blade Mining and Milling Company, popular with mineowners and miners alike, and that was the mark of a tremendous personality.

The record showed that Shores fought his own company to get cash settlements for miners killed or injured in the Yankee Blade. He donated a waterworks to the town. Some of the old fireplugs were still in evidence. He organized and led the Golden Eagles, a hose-cart company that wore uniforms like English grenadiers. Again, it was a measure of his vitality and popularity that the whole outfit was not laughed out of town.

They kept their hose cart in a shed on a little hill near the Yankee Blade mill, so that when the alarm sounded they could have a running start. Their regular meeting place was the Nose Paint Saloon, where presumably they discussed fire-fighting techniques along with other weighty problems, and that was where they were one night when a cafe caught fire.

It was said that they were in a somewhat exhausted and befuddled condition by the time they sprinted to the hose cart. They started their brave run but they got a little off the smooth, narrow trail coming down the hill and ran the outfit into the Yankee millpond. Someone put the cafe fire out with buckets while the Golden Eagles floundered in the water, grenadier hats all afloat, and the girls from Grace Bond's house came down to fish them out.

Shores made a statement to the press: "Some scoundrel had put a smaller wheel on the left side of the cart." It was not true, of course, but the miners loved him for it.

Pictures showed P. R. Shores as a slender, dark-haired man with the devil flashing in his eyes. He was married to a beautiful woman, the daughter of a banker. Their carriage teams of glossy bays and the carriages themselves were said to be the finest money could buy, and the driver was always uniformed.

Freehanded, spectacular, always ready for a drink or brawl, Shores streaked across the mining scene when most of the camps were fading. After the Yankee Blade played out, he and his wife made a grand tour of Europe, and then he settled in the East, going into the banking business with his father-in-law.

Another, of course, was old Stony Jackson, who, when he was not telling mineowners the painful facts about their properties, spent his time fishing, or scrambling over Hellsgrin, driving pins into the ice and making minute calculations of the heave and flow of the glacier.

He was a shadowy figure there on the edge of the firelight, a huge man in corduroy coat and high boots. A black spade beard, hard and doubting eyes; and behind him stood Bolivar, the old white burro that never damaged a transit on a thousand miles of mountain trails.

There was Dealer Dan Powell, the handsome gambler from Queenie's place, who kept two blooded race horses in an insulated stable near the creek. When games were slow, he went down to pet the animals. He kept a veterinary in business fretting over them, and he had a groom to brush and coddle them; but no one ever rode them in a race.

When Dealer Dan disappeared as if by magic after shooting a man over a gambling bet, possession of the horses became a red hot issue between Queenie and some of Dealer Dan's creditors. The groom solved the problem by stealing the horses and getting away clean by way of Volcano Pass.

Alonzo Pike was there, but he was the most shadowy of all the ghosts, for he was Bennion's grandfather. The view of him was filtered through the impressions of his daughter, Bennion's mother. It could not be very sharp because Pike's daughter was only five when her father disappeared.

The normal way of building memories of a loved person is to remember little accurately and create much. Bennion was sure that his mother had followed such a pattern unknowingly. To her, Alonzo Pike had been a sandy-haired god. She even pictured him five inches taller than he actually had been. Later, he became a martyred saint.

Bennion had to fumble through the best way he could to make his own estimate of his grandfather. There was not much to go on because the people who had known Pike were scattered far and wide by the time Bennion began to take hard interest in a grandfather he had never known. Unlike many other men of Basin City's booming years, Pike was not one to attract attention in the newspapers.

He was superintendent of the Yankee Blade mill. Sometimes his name was mentioned when he went to a meeting of the Basin City Literary and Debating Society, and that was about it. He never fell into the millpond with the Golden Eagles, or shot up Queenie's place, or broke the faro game at the Nose Paint.

What did bring Alonzo Pike plenty of notice was the fact that on Friday night, April 2, 1909, when the wind was blowing snow wildly about the basin, he cleaned out four months' run of gold pig bars from the Yankee mill, loaded them on a strapping jackass named Whingding, and stole up the Hellsgrin Trail.

He escaped as neatly as the groom who stole Dealer Dan's horses, or he fell into the great crevasse at the head of Hellsgrin. You could take your choice because no man knew the facts.

Many thought they did. Witnesses, three of them not unreliable, reported seeing Pike and a burro sneaking around the town of Randall, over the mountains, the next evening after he left Basin City. They were quite positive. Their testimony was never proved or disproved. During the years after Pike's disappearance, he was reported in a hundred places.

Pinkerton men searched for him. The Yankee Blade Company offered five thousand dollars reward for information leading to his arrest. Based on the monthly averages of gold recovery at the mill, the amount he had taken was close to ninety thousand dollars, P. R. Shores reported.

"I never had the least doubt about his honesty," Shores said. "This comes as quite a shock. We are still investigating, and we have detectives on the job, but it looks like he did it."

Two people said it was impossible that Pike could have done such a thing. His wife said he just was not the kind of man to steal. Peleg Lockwood, foreman of the Yankee mill, said the same thing. His was a man's voice and he was respected, afterward becoming the superintendent of the mill.

The evidence could not be disputed.

Pike had borrowed the burro from Lucius Morgan. Six Golden Hoof miners, hurrying to shelter after coming off shift, saw him taking the burro to the Yankee mill. Its tracks were found the next day a short distance up Hellsgrin Trail. There were other marks, too, beyond those first ones, but blowing snow had made them unreadable.

Where a snowdrift lay across the trail near the head of the glacier, someone kicked up one of Pike's mittens. That snowdrift became a point of raging controversy because the great snow bridge that spanned the bergschrund was broken. Had Pike got the burro through the drift, or had he tried the snow bridge and plunged into the crevasse?

Even on the day following Pike's disappearance, men were able to wallow through the snowdrift. Some argued that it would not have been as bad the evening before. And the snow bridge—why, that was always building up and caving in of its own weight, as Stony Jackson later admitted.

Above the glacier, the rocky trail was bitterly wind-scoured and that very fact made it possible that a man and burro could have gone over it, although few men ever did use it in winter. No tracks were found above the glacier, but that was of no value, for when another burro was led up there, it left no marks on the flinty trail, and it was shod, while Whingding had been unshod.

There had been too much traffic on the road for Pike to have escaped that way; and the other trails were snow-blocked. If Pike had got away, it had to be by way of Hellsgrin Trail.

The Pinkerton men did not jump to conclusions. While some of them kept checking out the reports of Pike's appearance in various places far from Basin City, two others stayed in the town until summer. They searched the millponds, the bottoms of old prospect holes, unused drifts in the Yankee Blade tunnel, and the hollows where snow had lain in great drifts.

They checked out a great many things, working on the theory that unknown parties had robbed the mill safe, killed Pike and the burro, and contrived the appearance of his escape over the glacier trail. Popular opinion jeered that theory. Maybe Pike could have been forced to open the safe, but he had not been forced to borrow Whingding.

The two detectives in Basin City found nothing, as did their colleagues elsewhere.

Pike was deep in the glacier, or basking in the sun in Mexico or South America. Take your choice. After a hard winter in Basin City, with another one not far away, most miners inclined to the second opinion; it well suited their own wishful thinking.

Stony Jackson, who had been making his crusty reports to copper-mine owners in Arizona, returned after the excitement was all over. He gave the Yankee Blade a going-over and told Shores the mine was finished, and then he went back to his old love, Hellsgrin Glacier.

Late that summer he made his prediction about the body of Alonzo Pike. At first, the statement was received with awe. Imagine a man's knowing what was going to happen fifty years later! It was uncanny.

Then the doubts began to grow. Who knew that Pike was in the glacier, in the first place? Jackson's entire guess depended on that fact, and just because a snow bridge over Hellsgrin was broken, who could prove what had caused it to collapse? The weight of snow itself did that, especially in spring.

Jackson's conclusions about the broken bridge were based on previous winter studies of Hellsgrin and they were unintelligible to most, as were his mathematics of the movements of glaciers. He laid it down flat and let the scoffers have their field day. Jackson was an eagle and an eagle does not snap at gnats.

"A mighty safe guess," Queenie said. "None of us ain't going to be around to get our mitts on that gold in fifty years and see whether he's right or not."

The most widely favored statement made about Jackson's prediction came from Blackie Tedrow, who ran the Nose Paint. "Fifty years to move two miles? Why that's almost as slow as the goddamn' stage from Smelter Town!"

Bennion accepted the fact that not all who had been in Basin City in 1909 were dead, but with two exceptions, one of them extremely doubtful, he knew of no survivor of the time in question.

Stony Jackson died at his home in Estes Park in 1918. In the Capitol Building in Denver there was a picture of him, not because of his remarkable record as an engineer, or his glacier studies, but because he had become so rich through land investments in his last years that he could not be overlooked.

P. R. Shores was no man to die in bed. After he retired into the banking business in Philadelphia, he was almost killed in an explosion aboard a yacht. Then it was reported that he had been wounded in a bordello. Collecting rents, or some such thing. He drowned while swimming at Lido in 1921.

Blackie Tedrow, Queenie, Lucius Morgan, Homer Paden, and all the better-known residents of Basin City—they were every one accounted for. Dead.

The exceptions that Bennion knew about were Peleg Lockwood and Pancake Riddle. Lockwood was sunning away his remaining years at Bennion's ranch, his memory and his tongue still sharp and pungent. During fifty years he never changed his defense of Alonzo Pike: Pike would not have stolen. Someone else had taken those golden pigs. Maybe this unknown had gone out by the Hellsgrin Trail, dumping Pike's body into the crevasse on the way.

But Lockwood could not explain why Pike had got a burro. "How do I know? Maybe he wanted to drag a timber or some planks over at the mill. He was always fixing or doing something there after the rest of us had quit."

"He wouldn't have used a burro with a packsaddle and panniers to drag planks."

"I don't know, damn it! Nobody knows. Lonnie Pike didn't take them pigs. You can prove that when he comes out of Hellsgrin."

If he came out of the glacier. If he was ever in it. Bennion had searched so long and so hard amid the confusion that time puts on all events that he was not sure just what he did believe about his grandfather.

He got up and stood by the fire. While lying down he had been listening for the approach of other Theys, even though he realized it was highly unlikely that anyone would travel after dark.

Pancake Riddle. He was the other one who might be a living relic of Basin City's past. Old Pancake made and talked like the original prospector of all time. He had uranium claims from hell to breakfast and was always on the verge of a million dollar sale. To hear him tell it, he had had a personal part in every event of any note that ever happened during the mining era.

Pancake claimed to have been dealing a poker game in the Nose Paint during the winter of

1908–09. He knew all about the golden pigs at the Yankee mill. The trouble was that his theories and his facts, so called, contradicted each other in a hundred different ways.

Bennion walked through the freight yard to the street fence. He looked down at the Nose Paint. No light showed there. He was willing to bet that she was not asleep. Scared or not, she had made no sound to indicate that she was trying to bar the door from the inside.

Tomorrow, after the uncanny silence of the high-country night, after thinking the whole affair over, maybe she would be ready to talk more freely.

As Bennion went back to his fire he saw that the night had at last covered the pale slash of Hellsgrin.

THREE

Early morning sun worked its change on Basin City, warming to friendliness the drunken buildings in the swamp, taking the forlorn look from the gray wagons around Bennion, dancing on the shallow millponds.

He heard no sound from the Nose Paint.

Over there across the creek was where it had started. At home, he had a picture of the Yankee mill, in new gray paint, with its red tin roof, a plume of steam vapor standing above the whistle, and busy smoke rising from the tall boiler stack. That was long ago.

A change in the course of the creek had caused the stream to gnaw against the stone foundation at the bottom ledge of the mill. When that foundation went, the lower end of the structure collapsed and time had brought the rest of the mill sliding down the mountain in twisted wreckage. The boilers had dropped to creek level and were almost covered with silt.

Only one part of the mill showed any semblance of solidity, the rock safe room which stood on a ledge. It once had been connected by a strong walled passage directly to the furnace room where gold recovered by the flotation process was melted into bars for easy transportation. The old iron safe was still in the room, although no longer set into the thick rock wall.

To the right of the mill was the Yankee dump, a yellow fan spilling down to the creek, much eroded by rains and melting snows of half a century.

To the left of the top tier of the mill, the Hellsgrin Trail began, its lower switchbacks visible, the upper part—where it curved toward the glacier—lost against the rocks. Many times Bennion had walked over the whole area, as if trying by physical contact to wrest an answer from things inanimate.

He heard the singing. Someone was bawling out the ribald words of "The Muleskinner's Delight." And then in the midst of a line a hearty voice boomed, "John-ny! Johnny Bennion!"

It was old Pancake Riddle, coming in when the sun was barely up. He had seen Bennion's horses. Now he would assume that Bennion was in the Nose Paint, where the two of them had run into each other several times in summers past.

Once more Pancake broke out in song.

Bennion grinned as he walked over to the corner of the assay shop, squeezing into the narrow gap between the building and the fence. He did not show himself as he peered down the street. Smoke was coming from the stovepipe of the saloon. The door was closed.

Pancake and Sam Harding, the mouse-colored burro, were tramping up the street. Pancake's white whiskers made a fine bloom against the faded blue of his shirt. His sleeves were rolled above his elbows, showing his red wool undershirt. High laced boots with patched pants stuck into the tops. Police and Firemen's suspenders two inches wide.

He was smoking a black cigar. Pancake must have wangled another option payment on some of his uranium claims. Every now and then he caught a sucker.

"Damn' nigh caught him in bed, Sam," Pancake said to the burro, and then he marched up to the door of the saloon and thrust it open.

After that, Bennion was as surprised as Pancake.

There was a growl, a shout. Pancake reeled back from the door before the drive of a heavy black dog. Gail McBride shouted again and the dog stopped on the porch while Pancake staggered into the street against Sam Harding.

"Whoa there!" he yelled. "Call that monster off."

The woman came to the doorway. "It's all right, Saber. Sit." The dog sat down, obedient but tense, still growling low as he watched Pancake.

"What the hell, ma'am, what the hell!" Pancake stared at the woman. "Johnny, come out here!"

"He isn't in here."

"I seen his horses!"

43

It had gone far enough, Bennion thought. If he had known she had a dog, he would not have let it happen at all. He stepped into the street and called, "Hey, what's the matter over there?"

"A female with a fighting dog!" Pancake answered. "Get over here!"

"You're not hurt, are you?"

"One more chomp and I'd be damn' nigh et up," Pancake yelled. "When did you start keeping women around the premises?"

"Miss McBride is an honored guest," Bennion said. "Come on over to my camp and cool off."

Pancake had to take his burro the long way around. He came in the back side of the freight yard, a heavy-set old coot whose endurance in the mountains was remarkable, considering that he was well into his seventies. He began to unpack Sam Harding, talking as he worked.

"What's she doing in our saloon, Johnny?"

"Staying there."

"I seen that much! Did you tell her she could?"

"Not exactly, Pancake."

"I thought so! Country's going to hell, Johnny. I seen a jeep not two miles from here this very morning, and some flatlander has got a road dozed clean into the saddle this side of Volcano Pass. Some crazy uranium hunter—"

"That road goes to an aquamarine mine," Bennion said.

Pancake banged a frying pan down on the

wagon box. "You interrupt a man, Johnny. Aquamarine. Whoever heard of that? I was saying the country's going to hell. Roads everywhere, jeeps underfoot, and now a female wearing pants right in our own saloon. What's the matter, boy? She sic that dog on you and scare you into letting her stay there?"

"I didn't know she had a dog until you kicked it and stirred up all the ruckus." Bennion grinned.

"Kicked it! I was only going in like I always do." Pancake sheared the end of his cigar off and spat it from his beard. His teeth were still strong and white, and his brown eyes were sharp in their bedding of fine wrinkles. The flesh showing from his cheekbones on up was a healthy pink. "Look at that," he said. "Bit clean through my cigar when that pit dog come slashing at me."

"Had your breakfast?" Bennion was wondering how he had missed seeing the dog the day before.

"Hell no. You know I never eat until I've traveled five or six miles. It ruins a man's stomach to stuff it before he's had exercise. Don't invite me. I'll do my own cooking, thanks."

Pancake was a good cook, at that, one of the few men Bennion knew who could whip up a clean, well-done meal with a minimum of effort. Bennion sat down on the wagon box and watched Pancake go to work.

"Which way did you come in, Pancake?"

"Volcano Pass. When I hit Chapman Gulch I

could look over and see that new road sticking out like an outhouse in the front yard. Aquamarine. Christ!"

"Did you see anybody else headed this way?"

Pancake was mixing biscuit dough in a hollow in the top of a sack of flour. He gave Bennion a quick, hard glance. "No. Who was you expecting, Johnny?"

"I don't know." Unconsciously, Bennion looked up at the glacier.

"Oh! So that's it, huh?" Pancake shook his head. "Don't you believe a word of it, boy. Lonnie Pike ain't in that glacier. There's two places where he could be, in a crosscut I know about in Yankee Number Three, or right over there in a hole near the Golden Hoof. Now I tell you how I come to know. It was about—"

"You've told me, Pancake." That same story and a good many others, all of them conflicting.

"Suit yourself," Pancake said grumpily. He put his biscuits in the frying pan, put a battered lid on it, and began to rake coals from Bennion's breakfast fire around the sides of the pan and over the lid. "You mean it's getting on toward the time that engineer Johnson said Lonnie would come sliding out of Hellsgrin?"

"This is the year."

"Hard to believe." Pancake shook his head. "I'll swear it wasn't a week ago I was running the poker game there in Blackie Tedrow's place, down there where you let every stray woman in the country make free of things—Her and that wild wolf hound . . ." Pancake lost the thread of his thought for a while. "Anyway, old Karl Richmond come bustin' in and said Lonnie had grabbed all the gold from the Yankee mill and lit out. I said right then—"

"You told me, Pancake." Another version had Pancake eating breakfast with Joe Flager, general manager of the Golden Hoof, when the news of the robbery came. In still another version, he had been talking to Dealer Dan Powell down at the stable where Dealer Dan kept his race horses. The trouble with that last version was that Dealer Dan had been gone almost a full year before the robbery.

"Suit yourself," Pancake said. He began to cut bacon from a slab with a massive pocket knife. "Them as know the truth about things around here ain't listened to in nowise. Believe I will borrow your fry pan, Johnny."

"Help yourself." Bennion started toward the street.

"Put her in a dress like she ought to wear, instead of them pants, and she'd be a looker, sure enough."

"I've got other things on my mind, Pancake."

"Oh sure! If she'd let her hair grow out properlike, like the women in my day . . ."

Bennion kept walking.

47

"And tie that murdering wolf dog up . . ."

Pancake's voice followed Bennion all the way to the street.

The door of the saloon was open. Bennion did not see the Saber dog, so he whistled to give warning of his approach, and an instant later he heard the woman give some command to the dog. Bennion stopped in the doorway.

She was washing dishes on the stove at the back end of the room. He saw her sleeping bag on one of the bunks and a small duffel bag with personal effects on the bar.

"Come in, Mr. Bennion. I want to apologize for taking over your property, but I'll pay you whatever is right."

"Forget it." He walked slowly down the long room, keeping one eye on Saber. The bar and backbar were still intact, although badly stained from water. Along the east wall of the room was a collection of furniture, tables, chairs, a cherrywood secretary, and various pieces he had found in the town and stored here.

At the back was the door to the storeroom, a log addition with an inner wall of planks and a foot of sawdust as insulation between the two walls.

Gail McBride turned from the stove. "I've changed my mind about your offer to help me with the jeep. I'd like some help to bring it on down."

"Sure," Bennion said. To hell with Pancake's opinions; he liked the look of her hair, her trim, long-legged appearance in jeans.

"As soon as I finish these dishes, I'd like to go after my jeep, if you don't have something else to do, Mr. Bennion."

"Not a thing." Bennion sat down at a poker table. "Call me Johnny. Everyone else does." Absently he toyed with the handle of the take-off drawer under the table. Once there had been a slot in the table in front of the dealer, where he could drop the house's percentage of each pot into the drawer. Someone who had camped in the saloon before Bennion owned it had plugged the slot with a piece of pine inlay.

The woman went back to washing dishes. "My name is Gail."

"Fair enough." She was so coolly matter-of-fact that Bennion realized she was not giving any ground.

"Who's your friend with the burro?" she asked.

"Pancake? Just a prospector of sorts. I've known him for a long time."

"Oh? How long?"

"Five or six years, I guess. He pokes all around the Flying Horses in the summer and winters somewhere in New Mexico."

"I see." Gail rinsed the dishes with boiling water from a heavy, square copper teakettle. "I didn't know there were any prospectors like him left. What's his last name?"

"Riddle. L. G. Riddle."

"And that's all you know about him?"

Her words put Bennion on the defensive. What more was there to know about a windy old-timer who claimed to have been around when Rome was built. Pancake baffled knowing by the velocity of his conversation and the variety of answers given to the same question.

"That's about all," Bennion said. What was she trying to do, make him suspect a harmless windbag like Pancake? Idly he pulled the take-off drawer part way open, then closed it, and then he hauled it out quickly and stared for an instant.

A stub-nosed magnum pistol and a box of ammunition lay in the drawer.

Gail flipped a dish towel off a nail beside the stove. She turned toward Bennion as he folded his arms and closed the drawer with his knee. "I'll be ready in a minute," she said.

She was fairly ready now, Bennion thought, what with that hidden pistol and the dog. Well, you couldn't expect a woman to walk into the situation with only her looks and her sex as protection.

They walked down the Sorrowful in the bright sun. The black dog cruised the willows ahead of them. Part Labrador, Bennion guessed, crossed with maybe Newfoundland. Pancake would have said St. Bernard.

"Is this the part of the town that burned in 1910?" Gail asked, as they passed a stone foundation that showed the flaking effects of fire.

"From here clear up the creek almost to the Golden Hoof mill. It wiped out most of the town, but it was about dead by then anyway."

They crossed the creek on a rotting bridge stringer above the beaver ponds and went on to the toe of the steep slope where the jeep showed like a small green bug above the cliff. Bennion said, "Have you considered getting out of here, once you've got the jeep down?"

"At the worst, I could winch my way up this hill by burying something to tie to, but I think there's an easier way off to the left."

"Yeah," Bennion grunted.

Gail gave him a half-smile. "Men don't care too much to see a woman self-sufficient, do they?"

Bennion grunted again when they climbed the mountain and he saw how close the jeep was to the cliff. There were scarcely two wraps of cable left on the winch. "What do you figure now?" Bennion asked.

"I'll pull back into the timber and turn around. Then I'll get as far to the right of the cliff as I can and come down forward, with the winch run back under the jeep to hold. When I get past the cliff, I think I can go on down without the winch."

"You're going to drive it?"

"Of course. I came this far, didn't I? All I'm asking you to do is to hook the winchline for me."

Bennion looked down the hill. It was not his idea of a place to put a jeep. While he was debating, Gail started the vehicle and began to pull uphill. The first part of her plan worked well. She came down with the line strung under the jeep and back to a tree.

When the cable was extended almost its full reach, she stopped and slacked off the line. Bennion held his breath while he wondered if the jeep would hold. It stuck to the slope while he freed the line and tied into a jutting rock. She took the slack in and then once more began the slow descent.

Even with the changed angle of descent, she had to swing to the side to get around the cliff. The cable sawed into the gray talus, whipping across the surface as she fought her front wheels around. She went slowly over a buried boulder and Bennion saw daylight under the right front wheel and the left rear wheel.

The jeep settled in and came around straight. Bennion was sweating. When the cable was almost used, she was well below the cliff. The rest of the way was not as steep as the upper slope, but it was still more than Bennion liked.

He plunged down to the driver's side of the

jeep and flung open the canvas door. "I'll take it the rest of the way. Get out."

Gail wet her lips. "I can do it. Untie the line."

"What are you trying to prove!"

"I came this far. I'll take it on down."

Bennion lifted the door out of its brackets and tossed it on the slope. "Shall I lift you out of there?"

"No. Just untie the winchline, please."

After a few moments Bennion climbed back to the jutting rock and threw off the line when she gave him slack. As he stood in front of the jeep, waiting to secure the hook when all the cable was back on the drum, the hood of the vehicle was as high as his shoulders.

Gail was even higher, looking down at him through the windshield with a pale, determined expression.

Bennion stepped aside. After two long, tense minutes, he knew she was going to make it. He watched her all the way, until she stopped on level ground near the creek. She was sitting quietly behind the wheel when he came down the slope with the door. "All right, you told me so," he said.

She gave him a quick smile and shook her head. "I wouldn't do that again for a sackful of diamonds."

Bennion saw the man while he was going around the jeep to get in. A rider with a packhorse in tow, just breaking into the basin from the head of Sorrowful Canyon. They were coming very slowly. He got in beside Gail.

He said nothing about it until they forded the creek above the old bridge. "There's four of us here now."

"What do you mean?"

He pointed down the road. She tried to look through the dusty rear window in the canvas top. Then she stopped the jeep and got out. The rider was about a half mile away. "Who is that?"

"No idea at all," Bennion said.

He waited for her to loosen up on the way back to Basin City, but she had nothing to say, except to thank him when she let him out in front of the Nose Paint. Saber, who had left them when they started up the mountain, was sitting on the porch.

"How'd I miss seeing that dog yesterday?" Bennion asked.

"Probably because he was ranging around in the mountains while you were watching me. He trailed me in later." Gail began to unload boxes of groceries and gear from the back of the jeep. Bennion carried one box to the saloon porch and she thanked him with a finality that said she needed no further help.

"See you," Bennion said, and went back to his camp. Pancake was coming through the tall grass near the creek, his chipped and ancient telescoping steel fishing rod in his hand.

"Got six," Pancake said. "That's enough for you and me for dinner. A man could catch a hundred over there, wasn't ·for that man-eating dog that kept slopping around everywhere I wanted to throw a hook. I ain't going to get along with that dog, Johnny."

Pancake dumped a canvas fish sack on the wagon box. He took off his old black hat and ran his forearm across his silvery white hair. It was stubbed off so short against his pink scalp that the top growth contrasted oddly with his bushy beard.

"Got you into a chore, didn't she? Never thought I'd see the day you'd help bring a stink wagon into our basin. I can remember when—"

"She didn't need much help, Pancake."

"Nope, Johnny, guess she didn't. She's got her help coming up the road right now. Would any man in his right mind think she'd come here alone, a woman like her, or any other woman? Hell no! She cased this place, that's what she did, looked things over to see how the cards was running, and all the time she had it cut and dried with that fellow coming up the road right this minute.

"She charmed you, Johnny, with them long legs and that walk and that black hair. She found out everything she could in advance and now her and her man are fixing to run things around here. I'll tell you—"

"She didn't try to charm me," Bennion said. "Not by a damn sight she didn't. You're talking like a wild man, Pancake."

"All right, all right!" Pancake waved his arms. "You'll see. It looks like everybody in the United States is piling in here to find something in the glacier that ain't there in the first place. What's going to happen around here when forty, fifty people get to sitting on Hellsgrin, looking sidewise at each other and waiting for a hundred thousand dollars' worth of gold to come sliding right out into their hands, and right in the middle of it that girl charming a bunch of greedy-guts men, working 'em against each other?"

"Charm hell!" Bennion said. "She acts more like she hates men. As far as forty or fifty people—"

"That's the way to work on a man. She knows. You don't go after something that's easy to get, Johnny. I'll tell you right now what I'm going to do, I'm going to get to hell out of here and go some place that ain't overrun with crazy people thinking a fortune in gold pigs is going to pop right out of Hellsgrin, if they just set there with a basket ready to catch it."

Pancake began to gather up his gear. "You keep these fish, Johnny. I'll get me some more up in Angel Park."

"What are you running away from, Pancake? A woman and a man that likely never saw each other before. Maybe no one else is going to show up. You generally stay here a week or two, so now you're letting a couple of strangers scare you out."

"I ain't lost nothing here." Pancake continued to slam his pack together. "Let's get out and let 'em sit on that glacier till they get rheumatism. Then we can come back and enjoy ourselves. Now where did I see Sam Harding last? Oh yeah, down there near your pasture fence."

Bennion didn't doubt that Pancake was leaving. It was not so much the things he had been raving about; he just did not cotton to flatlanders in the hills, unless they were prospects to buy some of his uranium claims, and then he only tolerated them.

"Take it easy, Pancake," Bennion said. "I like your company and I might need some help."

"If you get out of here, you won't." Pancake stopped packing and faced Bennion squarely. "Johnny, there ain't no gold in that glacier."

"I'm going to stay and find out."

"I know there ain't!" Pancake sawed the air with his arm.

"Prove it to me."

"I can't." All the pressure went out of the old man. "I don't know, like everybody else. Pay no attention to all those yarns I tell you, but one thing I'll swear—your grandfather ain't in Hellsgrin."

"How do you know?"

"A hunch. That's all, Johnny—a hunch." Pancake sighed. "And maybe that's like a lot of my other hunches. They work, and then again, they don't."

For just a while, all the harmless bombast was gone from Pancake, the contrariness that made him call Jackson "Johnson" when he knew better, and all the slam-bang positiveness about knowing things that others did not know, but it never lasted long, this meekness.

Now it was a hunch he had—and from there he would be off and running, full of sound, and dealing his multiplicity of stories from anywhere in the deck.

Pancake was—Pancake.

The horses were in the street. Bennion walked away to meet the new arrival.

FOUR

From the first glance Bennion disliked the man. He was big and heavy, a full-faced individual with a grizzled mustache. He reminded Bennion of Wingate, one of a group of elk hunters Bennion had brought into the basin three years before. Before that trip was over, Bennion had come to despise Wingate.

The man came up the street slowly, looking at the buildings. There was a rifle in his saddle boot. The saddle horse was limping, and the legs of both horses were badly cut.

Saber sat in the doorway of the Nose Paint. The rider divided his attention between Bennion and the dog after he stopped and got down stiffly. "Your mutt?" he asked.

"No," Bennion said. The man was tired and that had brought an offensive sort of irritableness to his features. At best, he would be an arrogant bastard, Bennion thought, loud and combative when drinking, pushing hard when sober. He was a second Wingate for sure.

"Is there a place fit to stay in?" the fellow asked. He looked at the Nose Paint.

"That's taken. You might try that one-story log with the false front down the street."

"I saw it. You the general manager around

59

here?" It was not quite an insult because the fellow tried to temper it with a grin. "My name is Tyner."

"Bennion." The packhorse was so tired it could not lift its legs to stamp away the flies swarming on its cuts and scrapes. Bennion took a quick look at the pack; it was expertly done.

"Where are *you* putting up?" Tyner asked.

"I'm camping."

Tyner looked up and down the street. "Any place you put in would be camping. If that cabin is so good, why aren't you in it?" Once more he skirted insult by grinning.

"Suit yourself. It's there." Bennion kept looking at the packhorse. Tyner never in the world had slung a job like that. "Those are Sandy Mulford's horses?"

"Yeah. What about it?"

"You came up the canyon?"

"Every miserable, stumbling, waterlogged foot of the way. I put in the best part of two days in that hellhole." Tyner's face leaped with interest when Gail came to the door. "Well!" he said, grinning.

Bennion watched them as they looked at each other. If there was recognition between them, he did not detect it. Gail sized up Tyner coolly, then turned back into the saloon. Saber left the porch and went sniffing through the weeds along the edge of the rotten sidewalk.

"Well!" Tyner said. "Yours? Oh, I forgot, you're camped out. Interesting little community you've got here, Bennion."

"I'll help you unload." Bennion kept fighting back his slow-rising temper as he looked at the packhorse.

Tyner settled on the log house. He kicked the door open and looked inside. "This will do fine, although I wouldn't want to buy it as an investment." He came back to his horse and got the rifle and a pair of heavily loaded saddlebags. "What's your line, Bennion?"

"Ranching."

"Cowboy stuff, huh? You must love TV. Ever get any of it out in this country?"

"A little more than we need." Bennion unlashed a sleeping bag from the top of the pack. He slipped the pack and eased it down and stood looking at the sweat-galled back of the packhorse. Under the packsaddle it was worse. "How come Mulford didn't send a man with you?"

"I didn't need anyone."

"This pack hasn't been off since you left the Bonnet."

"Right as a rabbit, cowboy! I'd never have got it back on if I'd taken it off."

"Two nights, huh?"

"Yep!" Tyner said cheerfully. He pulled the saddle off the other horse and dropped it, skirts down, on the ground.

"That's a hell of a way to treat any horse," Bennion said.

"Before you begin to bleed over it, let me say that I bought the horses from the bandit at that ranch, so I'd say it was none of your damn' business." Tyner tried to speak pleasantly, but it was like his smile, a thin layer over ugliness.

Up at the freight yard, Pancake cut loose suddenly with "Hogs in the Cornfield."

"Who's that?" Tyner asked quickly.

"Pancake, an old friend of mine."

"Another cowboy, huh?"

"Prospector."

"Hmn." Tyner dropped the bridle on the saddle. "A regular convention here. Does this happen every summer?"

"Sure. Sometimes there's forty or fifty people sitting up on Hellsgrin Glacier, all looking sidewise at each other."

"The hell!" Tyner tried to laugh it off when he realized the truth. "You're kidding, of course," and then he had to look at the glacier, as if he had just become aware of its existence.

"That's it, Tyner, Hellsgrin Glacier."

"Yeah." Tyner made a long word of it. "I always thought they were sort of flat, but that thing is hanging in the air."

"The upper part, what you'd call the névé, I guess, is considerably flatter."

"Névé, huh?" Tyner stared at Bennion. "I just

might go up and take a look at it while I'm here." He kept studying Bennion. "You're local, huh? You come here all the time?" He implied that Bennion thereby held some great advantage.

"If you'll watch the horses I'll get 'em some oats."

"That's another thing, where do I tie these babies up so they won't run back to that ranch?"

"I've got a piece of fenced pasture on the creek."

"How much?" Tyner sighed as if he had been robbed ever since he came in sight of the mountains.

"Nothing." Bennion walked around the pack lying on the ground and went to the saloon, where Saber was back at his post, disputing passage. Gail had to call him off.

There was no window in the storeroom and the ventilator pipe in the roof, screened and hooded, gave scant light. Bennion left the heavy door open. It was cool and dry inside. Sometimes Bennion thought he could smell the odor of the barreled beer that had been stored here long ago.

Tracks in the dust film on the plank floor showed that Gail had looked things over, but nothing appeared to have been disturbed, the tools, the food supplies on wall shelves, and the miscellany of items Bennion had packratted from the town, including a roulette wheel he had found hidden under musty hay when he was wrecking an old barn for lumber.

He filled a five pound lard can with oats and went out to the main room. Gail was cleaning the top of the stove.

"Figuring on a long stay?" Bennion asked.

"I'm staying, if that's what you mean."

"Did you ever see the fellow who just showed up—Tyner?"

Gail shook her head. "You mean I should know him?"

"Nobody should know that guy," Bennion said, thinking of the horses. "Do you want to make a pool on how many more show up?"

"Hardly. I'm not interested."

"You'd better believe that. I don't." Bennion went out.

Tyner's horses were wandering away. Tyner was trying to carry the whole mass of his camping gear into the cabin in one motion and he looked as if he wanted help. Bennion went on past him and led the two horses down to the pasture with the bucket of oats.

His own horses tried to muscle in when they saw the bucket. They stood outside the fence and blew through their nostrils at him while he dumped the oats in a stone trough. He was examining the cuts on the legs of Tyner's horses when he heard the plane.

It came in from the east, a two-place blue job,

its shadow racing on the ground before it as if dropped low on the sunny side of the basin. That was the wrong side for this time of day and if the pilot came much lower, his only way out would be the canyon.

Bennion watched with an expert's judgment. The pilot realized he was too low and began to pull up, veering off toward the Flying Horses. He gained safe altitude, then banked below the head of the canyon and came rushing back on the south side of the basin, the engine drumming noise off the steep sides of the Granite Mountains.

He still could not make the saddle above the glacier, Bennion knew, but now he was high enough to go out easily over the canyon after he turned once more. That was not the pilot's intention. For a moment it appeared that he would crash into the rocks above Hellsgrin, but he made a tight turn and fought for more altitude.

The second time he circled up from the canyon he was high enough to get out to the east. Bennion listened to the noise of the engine going away. He could not be sure, but it seemed that the distant humming diminished, then increased, and then dropped off to silence with just about the right timing to indicate that the plane had landed, or tried to land, on Black Bear Mesa, six miles east.

You could put a plane down there if you had the guts and savvy and brought it in on the downhill slope, when you desperately wanted to land the other way because it seemed more natural and safer. Bennion went up the street.

Tyner was sitting in the cabin doorway, drinking fruit juice from the can. "Was that a local plane?" he asked.

"No," Bennion said.

Tyner finished the juice. He threw the can into the street and wiped his mustache with his hand. "Are you sure you'd know, or are you one of those Flying Farmers?"

Bennion went back to his own camp. Pancake was trying to get Saber to come to him and take a biscuit from his hand. The dog was standing ten feet away. "Look at him!" Pancake said. "Me trying to be friends, even after he did his best to mangle me."

"Maybe he only eats live meat."

Pancake tossed the biscuit. Saber let it drop on the ground, sniffed at it and walked away. "Look at that!" Pancake said, outraged. He retrieved the biscuit and put it back on the wagon box under his frying pan. "The hell with him. He can starve."

"Maybe he's been trained not to take anything from strangers."

"Stranger! I ain't no stranger to him, not after he damn' nigh et the hind end off me. Oh, he's been trained all right. I seen he pretended he didn't know that fellow that just showed up, but did you notice the way that Gail girl stared at him? She knowed him, sure enough. The two of them are working the biggest badger game you ever got into. Mark my words, Johnny—"

"They don't know each other, Pancake."

Pancake snorted. "That's it, that's it! Let a skirt swish by a young fellow like you and he goes plumb blind."

"She hasn't got any skirts."

"Hell with you, Johnny. I should've left you when I started to, and then I got to thinking of you here alone with that pair of badger-game artists. Besides, why should they scare me out? I was here before they was born."

"Suit yourself about leaving, Pancake. If you're scared of something."

"Me scared! Me scared of a woman and a fat and dirty greenhorn!"

Bennion grinned. "Fat and dirty. You sound like you played football once, Pancake."

"Never seen a game of it, except on television. Don't listen to me if you don't want to hear the truth, that's all I got to say. Now let's fry them fish and quit worrying about something that ain't so in the first place."

Saber returned to watch them eat, lying well away from the camp, showing interest, but refusing scraps.

"Trained is right," Pancake growled. "She sent him over here to spy on us, and that's just what he's doing. Dogs can do most anything, I'll tell you. I remember Gassy Thompson's dog in Cripple Creek. Big brindle bull, he was, by the name of Sulphide. Gassy used to send him to rush the growler, and a sight it was to see him carrying that tin beer bucket, with his teeth showing, and maybe slobbering some in the bucket as he trotted.

"Sulphide developed an appetite for beer. Got so he no sooner got out of the saloon than he slipped around in the alley and lapped up half the beer, and then he'd go home. Gassy kept changing saloons, thinking the bartenders were taking advantage of Sulphide. He was scrapping with half the bartenders in Cripple Creek before he caught Sulphide in the alley drinking the beer.

"Old Gassy twisted the bulldog's ears to punish him. You think that cured Sulphide of drinking? Hell no. He went right on lapping it up, but every time he'd stop at a water trough and hold the bucket under the pipe until it was plumb full again before he took it home. You think dogs ain't smart? Ha!"

Thereupon, Pancake crawled into the wagon box where the bedroll was and proceeded to take a nap, while Bennion washed the cooking utensils.

The damned old cuss, Bennion thought, grinning to himself. And then he began to worry about the plane.

Say it had made a successful landing on Black Bear Mesa. Six miles. The occupants could reach Basin City before sundown with no strain.

Pancake began to snore so loud, with such a horrible choking, rattling noise, that Saber got up and edged closer, stiff-legged, growling in a puzzled tone. Bennion held his hand out slowly. "Come here, Saber."

The dog eyed him steadily, then growled and jumped back.

Pancake sounded as if he was settled in to sleep all afternoon. Bennion looked up at his unfinished drift fence. That's where he should be, but he did not feel like it.

Instead, he went down the street. He was past the green jeep when Gail came to the saloon door with a broom. Bennion stopped and turned back, "Mind if I borrow your jeep to run down the creek for a few minutes?"

"Yes," she said, "I do mind."

"Thanks." Bennion went on.

Tyner came to the door of his cabin, holding a canteen cup full of steaming coffee. "What now, cowboy?"

"I'm going after some balsam gum to put on your horses' legs. You want to come along?"

"No thanks. Horses are your department." Tyner laughed.

The first stand of Alpine firs was a mile below town. Bennion gathered pitch in a rusty tin can and went back to the pasture, where he built a small fire to melt the gum. It was too early, but yet he kept looking up toward Hellsgrin Glacier and the saddle to the left of it.

That plane could have got in a lot of trouble if the pilot tried to land uphill.

With the warm pitch he treated the cuts on the two horses. The packhorse was really chopped up, and now it was going lame in both forefeet. Bennion pressed hard where the taper of the hoof ran into hair. Both feet were sore, but there were no bad cuts and the shoes were soundly fixed.

It was not good; if it was what he suspicioned, the horse was going to be in bad shape by the next day. He led the animal down to the creek and forced it to put its feet in the icy water.

Whoever they were, if they came into that mesa the wrong way . . . Well, there was a fairly quick and easy way to find out.

Once more Tyner came to his doorway as Bennion went past with Stranger. This time he had nothing to say. Fat and dirty. That fitted just fine.

Pancake was still snoring when Bennion saddled and rode away.

FIVE

They were all watching Bennion by the time he reached the start of the Hellsgrin Trail above the Yankee mill. He saw Gail standing in the street, Tyner watching from beside an overturned buggy behind his quarters, and Pancake sitting on a wagon box in the freight yard.

Bennion led Stranger most of the way. It was a climb that would take him up nineteen hundred feet higher than the town by the time he reached the head of Hellsgrin. Basin City grew smaller. He went around the sharp-ribbed shoulder of the mountain and then he could no longer see the town.

It was cold, bleak granite, a narrow trail with loose stones in it, a cold wind whipping around the corners.

He came to the glacier. It lay below him, heavy snow masses settling lower to be compacted by their own weight into ice that would flow in sweeping curves, first to the north, and then around to the west. From where he was, Hellsgrin did not look like a cliff glacier because the down angle of the view deceived. The last great curve could not be seen from the trail, that last part that was a sheer icefall, but there were many other icefalls cut from view by the curves of the

71

gorge and Bennion knew from hard experience how dangerous it was to try to scale any of them. There was only one place on Hellsgrin where a man could walk about easily, just above Point 7 where the ice for a short distance had only a five degree pitch.

Bennion stopped where the controversial snowdrift had lain across the trail fifty years before. Just the flip of a stone away, the great snow bridge had angled out to span part of the arc at the head of the glacier. Pike Bridge, Jackson had called it in his writings after 1909.

Bennion had copies of his pictures of the bridge, taken before and after that date. They were, understandably enough, amazingly like the pictures Bennion had taken during every winter since 1954.

The same stone flipped out to touch the vanished bridge would spin down to a steep snow slope finned with dark rocks, and that was the gathering funnel that sucked everything toward the scythe-curved crevasse known as the bergschrund.

It gaped down there, snow-edged on top, glinting blue and hard inside the soft white lips, wide enough to receive a small horse.

Men who had never seen Hellsgrin in winter, or even in summer, had asked why someone had not immediately probed into the bergschrund when it was thought that Pike and Whingding had fallen into it. They spoke without knowing of the masses of snow that lay soft and smothering deep at the head of the glacier in winter, and without knowing that the snow bridge itself had weighed fifty tons or more.

Summer or winter, the bergschrund was an ancient enemy. In its lower depths it worked, closing like a gigantic crusher, impacting snow that fell into it, impounding in the ice for more than half a century everything that entered.

Jackson had been along the edge of it on a rope, measuring, observing. His Point Zero was visible where the sheer drop from the trail met the snow slope, a piece of rusted drill steel embedded deep in the granite. Bennion had been that far down, and did not care to go any farther.

Blunt, arrogant, that prediction of Jackson's. He did not qualify by saying, *"if Pike is in the glacier."* His statement said that Pike *was* there and *would* reach a certain point on a given date. Looking down at the great crevasse, Bennion wondered as he had often wondered before, had Jackson known facts that no one else knew to make him so sure? If he had, he had never, to Bennion's knowledge, revealed them to anyone.

But Jackson had not been in Basin City when Pike disappeared.

As Bennion watched, a tiny rock rolled down the snow beside the trails of other bits of granite, one little fragment of rock from a mountain fourteen thousand feet high, rolling on a snowbank, dropping silently into the waiting bergschrund.

In fifty years would that mite of granite appear almost two miles away? Bennion went on up the trail.

A half mile more was enough to give him the altitude to see Black Bear Mesa. No dark spot anywhere on the brown field of grass. He looked with binoculars. The firs around the mesa grew larger, and from this vantage the field appeared to be one unbroken gentle slope. It gave the same deceptive appearance from the air too.

Suddenly he ducked under Stranger's neck and moved back to steady the glasses on the saddle. There near the lower end of the mesa, over against the trees. A growth of some kind that blended against the firs, but did not fit the general height of the trees.

The breathing of the horse kept throwing the field of vision up and down. Bennion stepped away and sat down, steadying his elbows on his knees as he held the glasses. It was not natural growth, that bump at the edge of the timber. He caught the faint, pale gleam of metal, just a sliver showing in the dark green.

It took a long time to work around the rocky spurs of the mountains that lay between him and the mesa. It was a blue plane, a badly wrecked plane, and someone had tried to conceal it from air view by piling spruce boughs on it.

The man was lying on the needle mat just inside the timber. Twisted aluminum, jagged, razor sharp, had done a frightful job on him, but when Bennion felt his wrist, he found it warm. For a few minutes Bennion thought he was still alive. No, he was dead. He might have died just minutes before; it could not have been very long.

There was no evidence to indicate that his companion had tried to help him in any way. Cards in the dead man's wallet said he was a licensed pilot, Walter N. Baker, Pasadena, California.

A blue, two-place plane. From the seats forward the interior was a mess and it was hard to believe that the passenger could have walked away, let alone put in all the work of chopping boughs to hide the plane. From the scattered gear inside, Bennion took a down sleeping bag and covered the dead man.

He walked down the mesa. The lower part was twice as steep as the slope above, and that was what deceived you. The plane had not flipped, which indicated that at the last moment the pilot had realized he was going into a bad slope, and had tried to get his nose up.

But he had caught a wing tip against the ground, the plane had slewed around, still right side up, and then had crashed with fearful force against the base of the trees.

Bennion went back and examined the radio

again. It was a waste of time. With angry deliberateness he tore the boughs from the plane and hurled them into the forest, so that the bright parts of ripped metal showed, and then he worked the worst damaged wing up and down and from side to side until it tore loose. He dragged it out on the mesa where it would show clearly from the air.

A half mile north of the plane, he struck the trail to Basin City. The survivor's tracks were there, and they led all the way to the ghost town.

Pancake was trying to keep supper warm. "Where you been, Johnny? Leaving me here with people coming in from all directions, and that Gail girl and Tyner taking up thick as thieves the minute you was out of sight, and—"

"How many came in?"

"Well, there was one, anyway one. There's probably forty or sixty more on the way," Pancake grumbled.

"Did you see the man who came down the east trail?"

"Yeah, I talked to him." Pancake set a pan of warm water on the wagon box. "Wash your paws and let's eat. I been half starved waiting for you. Yeah, I talked to the fellow. Sort of likable, you might say. He walked in from Randall. His name's Deadwood, or some such."

"What did he have to say?"

"Not much. He come limping in about an hour ago. Hurt his knee when he fell in the rocks."

"Where is he now?"

"He's staying with Tyner." Pancake raised his hand and shook his head. "No, they didn't know each other. I seen that much when they met. I could tell they was strangers, but that Gail girl you're so high on . . .

"No sooner were you out of sight than they ran for her stink wagon and headed for Hellsgrin. They didn't get very far up the hill." The last fact seemed to please Pancake.

"It's anybody's glacier," Bennion said. "Did they go clear up?"

"Naw, just poked around the lower part."

Bennion began to eat. After a while he would go down and have a word with Deadwood.

He did not have to go. The man came to the freight yard a half hour later. He was about Bennion's age, about five feet ten, a square-shouldered, trim-looking blond with a very short haircut. He was limping.

"I'm George Durwood. I've already met your partner here, Mr. Riddle. You're Bennion, the man who owns the whole area?" Durwood's eyes were blue and frank.

"I'm Bennion, yes."

Durwood grinned. "So you don't own the whole country? I got my information from Tyner, who got it from McBride, and that goes to prove how things grow."

"McBride?" Pancake said. "Where's he?"

"He means Gail," Bennion said.

Pancake grunted. "Hell of a way to say a woman's name."

Durwood sat down on the wagon box, straightening his left leg carefully. "I sort of jammed the knee, or something, when the plane cracked up."

"Plane!" Pancake said. "I thought you walked in."

"I did—from the plane." Durwood's features were strongly formed, heavy cheekbones, sturdy jaw, eyes well protected by strong brows. It was a pleasant face in spite of that, lightened by mobility of expression.

"Your plane is more than cracked up," Bennion said. "How did you get out of it?"

"I'm afraid of flying. When we started to land, I was stretched out behind the seat, with sleeping bags and packs and everything else I could find jammed around me. The jolt doubled me up, in spite of that."

"Was the pilot alive when you left?" Bennion asked.

"From a medical standpoint, perhaps yes. I couldn't do anything for him. Five doctors on the spot couldn't have helped him one bit. He wasn't suffering, Bennion."

That was all undoubtedly true, but the point

stuck in Bennion's craw. A man in shock might have run away from the plane, not responsible for his actions: but Durwood had not been in shock. He had been in deliberate control of himself and he had walked away from a dying companion because he was in a hurry to get to Basin City.

"You didn't file a flight plan?" Bennion said.

"No." Durwood rubbed his knee. "Look, I wanted to come in here like all the rest of you, with as little attention as possible. I'm sure that every one of us was hoping no one else would be here. On impulse I had Baker circle the basin just to see if anyone was here. When I saw the horses and the jeep, I guessed there must be a dozen people here, but I kept hoping that maybe part of them were fishermen or uranium hunters—or something.

"Then we crashed. Instead of starting a big air search and rescue deal, I chose to cover the plane. One week from now, a month, or a year—what difference will it make to Baker?"

"How about his family?" Bennion asked.

"He had a cousin he hadn't seen or heard from for years. That was it. He died in a plane crash—Baker, I mean. All flyers live on the edge of that and he was no exception. He kept saying mountain flying was damned tricky. After we smacked into those trees, he was in no pain, I can tell you that for sure.

"I pulled him out. Sure, I could have held his

hand and stayed there. What for? I wanted to get to Basin City, and in spite of those Geological Survey quadrangles you no doubt saw in the plane, I wasn't sure where I was, so I left while there was time to get here before dark. If I hadn't covered the plane, somebody would have spotted it from the air. Then a ground party would have found my tracks and thought I was an injured survivor wandering in the mountains.

"I saved a lot of people a lot of time and expense, and I didn't hurt Baker a bit. When I go out of here, I'll report the crash, and lead a party in, if that's necessary."

Logical, straightforward—and cold-blooded; there was no fatty tissue in Durwood's head. He evaded nothing. That much was on his side, Bennion admitted.

Durwood kept shifting weight. "I came here for the same reason the rest of you did, to see if three hundred pounds of gold arrives in Hellsgrin at a point and time when my grandfather predicted."

"You're Stony Jackson's grandson?" Bennion said.

Durwood smiled. "I just said so."

Pancake grunted. He studied Durwood narrowly.

"And you?" Durwood asked Bennion.

"Alonzo Pike was my grandfather."

"Ah! That puts the personal, sentimental touch into the affair for both of us, doesn't it? The third generation trying to check the tangled doings of long ago. Romantic. Tell me, Bennion, are you more interested in finding the gold or in recovering Pike's body?"

"I'm interested in both," Bennion said evenly.

Durwood nodded as if pleased with the answer. He tipped his head toward the street. "Who are they?"

"We don't know."

Durwood looked at Pancake. "And you are just a casual visitor to old scenes, eh?"

Pancake did not answer. He stared at Durwood as if he had great doubts about him.

Tyner's laughter, loud and confident, came from the saloon.

Durwood glanced toward the street, then back at Bennion. "I got the impression they were together. When I was coming down the mountain, they were just leaving the glacier. Then Tyner told me he never saw the woman before."

"How come you threw in with him?" Bennion asked.

"I was looking for a shack to stay in, that's all. Maybe I forced myself on him, but I didn't feel like cleaning up one of the other shacks and he had plenty of room."

Tyner laughed again. He was having a splendid time over there in the Nose Paint. "I don't think they knew each other before," Bennion said. "Pancake does. What's the difference if they did?"

"None." Durwood looked at Pancake. "One thing I'd like to know—can a burro actually carry three hundred pounds?"

"Yes," Pancake said, "a good one can, easy. Whingding was a big, strong stud."

"Oh! You were that close to things, were you?" Durwood asked. "In spite of the costume, I didn't think—"

"Costume!" Pancake flared. "Why you damned young whelp! I'm eighty-two, and I ain't wearing no costume!"

"Sorry." Durwood held up one hand in a placating gesture, his eyes twinkling at Bennion. "I just thought you didn't look old enough to have been here in the early days."

"Said I knowed your grandfather, didn't I? If I don't look as old as I am it's because I took care of myself. Stayed out of aereoplanes, for one thing. I'll likely outlive you." Pancake stamped over to the firesite and turned his back, looking across the creek at the old mines.

Durwood shrugged, grinning at Bennion. Down the street, Tyner laughed again. "He makes his own comedy," Durwood said wryly. "His own peculiar sort, that is." He put his weight on both legs, testing his knee. "Five people here. There's two alliances, down there, and you and Pancake. That sort of leaves me on the edge."

Bennion said nothing.

"At the risk of sounding like a rheumatic old

man, I've got to put this knee to bed. Come down and visit me, if you've got nothing to do." Durwood limped away. He looked like a solid, tough little pro halfback going to the bench to rest.

"I don't care for him," Pancake said. "He's a bad oyster, Johnny. Stony Jackson didn't have no kids, as I remember."

"Yes, he did. He had two daughters, both of them born after he was getting along in years. I think Durwood is telling the truth."

"I wouldn't trust him as far as I can throw Sam Harding by a hind leg. Costume!"

Bennion looked up at Hellsgrin uneasily. The sun was gone. Above the Flying Horses, wind-whipped banks of clouds were crimson and some of their color was reflected on the glacier.

Technically, the gold belonged to the stock-holders, or their heirs, of the long defunct Yankee Blade Company, but Bennion had never given that legality more than token thought. Now, with five people here, and more likely to arrive, he had to adjust his thinking. The losers-weepers-finders-keepers philosophy was not going to work.

"Just suppose that gold does show up, Pancake. What do we all do then, sit up there on the ice and divide it? One bar for you and one for you and so on all around the circle until it's fairly split and everybody is happy?"

"You talk like a sky pilot," Pancake said. "You know better. People ain't changed one bit in fifty years, or fifty thousand either. Take a woman that'll drive a stink wagon clean over the Flying Horses by herself. You think she ain't hard as a rock? Take a man that'll walk away from a dying pardner, like that Deadwood did.

"Take Tyner—there's a cowardly bastard, if I ever seen one. He like to ruined his horses getting here. Maybe that was ignorance, but he's still a coward, and that's the most dangerous kind of fellow in the world.

"You think those kind of people will sit around and divvy up fifty thousand dollars all nice and easy? There'll be more blood than water running up there, if it came to pass that the gold was there, which it isn't."

"How about you and me, Pancake?"

Pancake poked Bennion in the chest. "We're not going to be fools, no matter what happens. Let's light out of here right now and let these crazy people go their best."

"You do what you want to, Pancake."

"Hell! You know I won't walk out on you." Pancake dredged in his pack and came up with two black cigars. "Damn gold anyway. Nothing but grief comes from having it, or from not having it." His voice was subdued, intense.

He held a firebrand to Bennion's cigar and the younger man studied his face. A strange, intelligent old duck, Pancake. The way he mixed his speech indicated that he could speak grammatically, if he wished, and the far places that he talked of at times made one wonder if he really had not been around and done many of the things he claimed to have done.

Certainly, he had not spent all his life tramping the mountains and deserts. Pancake claimed that he had made money a good many times during his life.

But he mixed so many whoppers with the things you might be inclined to believe that you could not be sure of any one thing he said.

"Take uranium, that's different," Pancake said. "These here cigars came from money spent by promoters who know as well as I do that there ain't nothing on the claims I optioned to 'em. They won't find nothing, they don't expect to. Only the rich idiots that put up the money will have any kick coming, and they already got more oil money than they can spend."

"Pancake, you keep saying my grandfather didn't go into that glacier. Do you know anything, or are you guessing?"

"Guessing," Pancake said simply. He pointed toward the Yankee Blade mine. "But I know a thing or two about that hill that those Pinkerton men didn't find out. We'll see."

There it was. One minute you could half believe him and the next instant he was as windy as ever.

"Your turn to do the chores," Bennion said. He walked out to the street and looked toward the pasture. It was a long-range diagnosis but he was sure of it: Tyner's packhorse was foundered.

From what he had seen yesterday and from the way the animal was standing now, with his front feet thrust forward and his rear feet pushed back, there was little doubt about it.

Mildly irritated by the delay of knocking, waiting for Gail to speak to Saber, and then having to explain, Bennion went to the storeroom. He took a pair of pincers and another bucket of oats.

"I know I'm a nuisance, being here in your way," Gail said. "Perhaps we could swap places with Tyner and—"

"We?"

"I mean I could trade buildings with them, if—"

"Stay here," Bennion said. "There's more room to entertain."

Gail looked at him angrily. "I didn't ask Tyner in here. I didn't ask him to go to the glacier with me either. He came along when I was putting oil in my jeep and—"

"No need to apologize to me." Bennion went out.

He stopped in front of the cabin and called to Tyner, who came out with a cup in one hand and a bottle of whiskey in the other. "Yeah?"

"Your packhorse is foundered. I'm going to pull his front shoes off."

Tyner's face turned ugly. "Foundered? You did that with the oats."

"You did it when you worked him to death in the canyon. He probably cooled off by standing belly deep in water, and then you left him two nights with the pack on. I didn't give him enough oats to hurt him."

"That's how horses founder, from too much eating. You think I'm dumb, cowboy?"

"Yes," Bennion said, and went on down the street. It was none of his business, but a horse could not be responsible for its ownership. He pulled the front shoes and led the horse down to the creek. When he went back up the street, Tyner was waiting, standing in the doorway with his rifle. His face was flushed with all the pushing ugliness that Bennion had suspicioned in him at their first meeting.

"All right," Tyner said, "you took his shoes off. Now he'll go lame when I try to get out with him."

"He was already lame. Shoes or no shoes, you couldn't get a mile with him."

"That's what you say, cowboy. You just traded horses with me when you tried to pull that little dodge. I'll take your packhorse in place of the one you ruined."

"Sober up," Bennion said. He turned away.

The bolt of the rifle clashed as Tyner threw a shell into the chamber. If Pancake had not said that Tyner was a coward, Bennion might have kept walking. When he turned to face Tyner, he knew it was well that he had. Tyner was trembling with rage, shaking and crazy mad enough to have done it. He cursed, foully, loudly, his voice rising.

"Get that packhorse of yours and sign him over to me right now, you sneaking sonofabitch!" Tyner yelled.

Bennion heard Pancake thumping down the street behind him. Without looking, he tried to wave him away.

"You hear me!" Tyner screamed. He raised the rifle.

Inside the cabin, Durwood said, "Put it down, Tyner." His voice was low and calm.

Bennion was ready to say he would get his packhorse; he was ready to promise anything that would give him a chance to get close to Tyner.

"Put it down, Tyner," Durwood said.

Tyner began to slip. He glanced sidewise. He turned his head slowly to look at Durwood. "I'm only trying to protect my rights!" he yelled.

"Over a horse, you'd kill a man. Get hold of yourself, Tyner." Durwood's voice was persuasive, and at the same time hard with purpose and authority.

Tyner lowered the rifle.

Bennion turned to meet Pancake. The old man was breathing hard from his run. "He was going to do it, Johnny."

"Yeah, he was."

Pancake got mad as they walked up the street. "You should have left his damn' horse alone!"

"Yeah."

"It wasn't none of your business! You don't like him and so you got stubborn!"

"That's right, Pancake."

"I told you he was a stinking coward. Why don't you listen to me? I've seen more killings over nothing than you'll ever read about."

Bennion threw his cigar away. "We're even on one thing. We've both been so scared that we bit a cigar in two."

Pancake laughed. He whacked Bennion on the shoulder. "I like you, Johnny! You and me could've pried up hell and put a chunk under it back in the old days."

"We may get that chance yet," Bennion said.

As they approached the Nose Paint, Gail called, "Johnny, may I see you for a minute?"

"Johnny, huh," Pancake muttered. "Pay her no mind, boy. What Tyner can't cook up, she will."

"See you, Pancake." Bennion went toward the saloon. He was still carrying the oat bucket and the pincers.

SIX

They drank coffee at the poker table with the take-off drawer. Working his knee lightly up and down to lift the drawer in its guides, Bennion decided that the lack of weight proved the gun was no longer there. The room was pleasantly warm after the chill of the street. She had cleaned it about as much as it could reasonably stand.

From its wire hook in the ceiling near the stove the gasoline light was hissing, ineffective yet in the mellowness preceding dusk.

"First stage," Bennion said. "We lack only the wine and soft music."

Gail eyed him steadily. "You can leave any time you wish if you think this is a seduction scene."

"I'll make that decision later."

"I didn't ask Tyner in here, until he knocked and invited himself. He had a bottle and insisted that I have a drink. This afternoon he hitched a ride with me when I started toward the glacier, and that was his idea too."

"Fine! You hate Tyner."

Gail held her anger down. "Keep that up and I'll hate you too." She went to the stove for more coffee, and Bennion observed that she had patched the tear in the seat of her jeans.

He watched her come back down with the light

behind her. Nice, he thought, very nice.

"Bill Tyner is the nephew of one of the original stockholders of the Yankee Blade," Gail said. "All he knows is what he's heard from relatives. He runs a used car lot in Ohio."

"Shoots 'em if they don't trade."

"That's not so funny. I saw what happened. Tyner is a man who should never drink."

"I'm with you there." Bennion could see himself and the woman in the backbar mirror, her dark head bent slightly toward him, two people sitting in a place that time had passed, two people struggling toward something from the long ago. "So we allow Tyner some technical right to any gold which may be in Hellsgrin."

"No. The interest that his aunt had in the Yankee Blade was bought out in 1913."

"On that basis, scratch Tyner, and me, and Pancake. How about Durwood and you?"

"All I know about Durwood is that I saw him when he came." Gail sipped her coffee.

"He's Stony Jackson's grandson."

"Oh!" The woman's eyes widened. "Do you know, or did he say so?"

"I'll take his word." Bennion paused. "Yes, I believe him, but what's the difference one way or the other? Jackson's glacier papers are public property." They were in the files of the Colorado State Historical Society.

"I've seen them," Gail said, "as I'm sure you

have, but I was thinking that perhaps Durwood might have other information about Hellsgrin, something that came down through private papers in the family."

"He could have, but I doubt very much that Jackson withheld anything in his monograph on glaciers."

Behind the backbar, joists creaked and tin rattled faintly in the part of the Nose Paint that Bennion had walled off and left to ruin. Over there the gambling room and the dance hall and rooms on the second floor were rotting away. Gail listened and looked at him inquiringly.

Bennion shook his head. "That part of the building talks." Especially when the wind blew, as the evening breeze was running now. "So Durwood's interest is personal and sentimental, as he says, and greedy, like the rest of us, but he also has no legal right to the loot."

Gail was still listening to the lonely creaking in the other part of the Nose Paint. She smiled quickly. "That made me nervous last night."

"I've sometimes avoided this place too, not entirely because of the creaking."

She gave him a puzzled look. "You? A man like you?"

"Whatever that means, yes." To get back on course, he said, "We're down to you. What rights have you got that the rest of us don't have?"

"I'm the sole heir to the old Yankee Blade

Company. There never were many stockholders. After the mine was abandoned, one of my great-uncles had visions of re-opening it, so he bought up the outstanding stock. It came down to me, all legal, all intact."

Lying on the floor with his nose under the brass rail by the bar, Saber rose suddenly and went to the door. Gail let him out and came back to her seat.

"What was your great-uncle's name?" Bennion asked.

"Shores. He was a brother of the Peyton Shores who was general manager of the company. Victor Shores and some of the rest of my mother's family put up most of the money to develop the Yankee Blade."

Bennion leaned back in his chair. "I see. I would say that you have a right to the gold, legally, but we're not before a court. We're shut up here in the basin with no one but ourselves to make decisions. It may sound dramatic but the fact remains that we're the only law here, the five of us now, and whoever comes tomorrow and from then on."

"I realize all that."

"So does everyone else, in a different sense, maybe."

Gail watched him quietly. "Let's start with you. I say any gold in that glacier is mine."

She tried hard but a muscle in her throat

betrayed her and her voice was not quite steady.

"Suppose I say no?" Bennion said.

"That's what I'm trying to find out."

"Did you try with Tyner?"

This time she did not flare up. "He's not to be trusted."

"But I am?"

Gail took a deep breath and let it out slowly. "I'm trying," she said, "but you're as hardheaded as any man I ever knew. You weren't so bad until I refused to lend you my jeep. Did that do it?"

Bennion grinned. "That did ruffle my feathers."

"Would you have given me your horse to ride to the glacier?"

After a moment's thought, Bennion said, "No. But that's a little different. A horse and a jeep are two—"

"I know. I also know we're getting nowhere." A quick smile touched the corners of Gail's lips. "Maybe I should have tried the wine and soft music after all."

"I believe it would have worked."

She met Bennion's eyes for a moment only. "I settled on you for reasons I won't try to explain, except that I thought perhaps your interest in finding your grandfather might temper your ideas about—well . . ." She gave it up. "I don't know exactly what I'm trying to say."

"Alonzo Pike is only a name to me," Bennion said. "For what he was, or for what he did, I'd be stupid to feel any responsibility. Oh, I'll admit that I once had a childish ambition to clear his name, just how I had no idea. Now you're trying to say that I should feel guilty because of him. Well, I don't." That was not quite true.

"You *have* considered the possibility that he got away?"

Bennion nodded. "That would solve all our worries neatly, wouldn't it?"

"It would, but I think he's in the glacier. I've studied all those old Pinkerton reports over and over, and I can't find anything to prove that he got beyond the bergschrund."

They watched each other in silence. It had grown dark outside and now the light from the gas lantern was bright in the far end of the room, but the massive bar was in soft shadows that hid the weather stains and scars, and Bennion thought, Hundreds of men stood right there when the facts were fresh and new, and they chewed them over and argued, and arrived nowhere. Why go over it all fifty years later?

But he said, "Pancake doesn't think Pike ever got to the glacier."

Gail frowned. "You said you don't know much about Pancake."

"I couldn't trace his life history, no. Otherwise, I think I know him." Bennion would never forget that Pancake had run down the street, unarmed, actually unable to help against Tyner, but still

95

he had come; and afterward, the measure of his concern for Bennion had been in the relieved and angry way he had upbraided him.

Gail said, "The old man, Peleg Lockwood, who lives at your ranch—has he talked to Pancake?"

"I see your research is sound. You know about Peleg. Yes, he and Pancake have talked to each other."

"Did Lockwood know him?"

"After they had talked of names and events in Basin City, Lockwood thought he remembered Pancake. Who are you hinting that Pancake really is?" Bennion asked.

"Did Lockwood recognize him?"

"Not right off. Lockwood is almost blind, for one thing. Two men seeing each other after fifty years—what would you expect? Lockwood accepted him, let's say."

"Pancake of course had no doubts about Lockwood?" Gail's tone continued to cast doubt on Pancake.

"Lockwood had a prominent job here," Bennion said, "while Pancake was a drifting prospector. Who do you think Pancake really is?"

"If Lockwood accepted him, why shouldn't I?" Gail went to the door to let the dog in. Bennion pulled the take-off drawer out. It was empty.

"What do you do?" he asked, when Gail returned to the table.

"Architect's assistant. I do the tedious work.

San Francisco. Unmarried. Twenty-seven. Hobbies, skiing and my jeep."

"You didn't mention pistol shooting."

"I heard you open that drawer the first time you were here. No, I'm not an expert pistol shot. I put two boxes of shells through that gun on the way here, and that's my first experience with anything beyond a .22."

Bennion felt like a man who lunges hard at a closed door and then falls flat when someone opens it unexpectedly.

"The next question," Gail said, "is where did I find the courage to come here alone. I didn't plan on coming alone, but that's how it turned out. I was to meet a friend in Salt Lake." She hesitated. "He changed his mind at the last moment. After that I stalled two days, wondering whether to go ahead or not.

"I told myself perhaps you'd be the only one here. How did I know about you? The woman at the State Historical Society mentioned you several years ago when I was there studying Jackson's papers. Then I stopped in Randall and made a few inquiries. The general opinion was that you were not an ogre, rapist, escaped murderer, or down-and-out thief, so I came on."

Her explanation was convincing and she seemed at ease, but when the weary joists and rafters talked again in the dying part of the building, she jerked her head nervously toward the sound. "Do you think we'll have more people here?"

"I wouldn't want to guess."

"I suppose it's a question of how many know, and believe, what Jackson said."

"The trip in here will stop more than you think," Bennion said hopefully.

"I hope so."

A great deal of her reserve had disappeared during the talk. When she spoke again, the impression of genuine confiding was stronger than ever. "I went to the sheriff's office in Randall, with the idea of seeing what I could do about getting a court order, and perhaps deputies, to protect my right to the gold. The least I was going to do was leave word where I was going."

Bennion could see that picture. He knew that the sheriff was on vacation. The deputy in charge, loudmouthed Art Tremaine, would not have gone down well with Gail.

"The sheriff was gone," she continued. "An undersheriff, or something, was entertaining a bunch of loafers. I listened to him for a few minutes and decided I was better off not saying anything. When he finally got through telling stories and asked me what I wanted, I inquired about the fishing in the area."

"Yeah," Bennion said. "You made no mistake by telling that guy nothing."

Lying near the stove, Saber roused at the sound

of creaking in the building, and then he lay down again with a thump.

"We've been all around my original question," Gail said. "I want to know where you and I stand."

"I'll admit that the gold, if any, seems to belong to you. Are you asking me to stand off all comers to see that you get it?"

"You make it sound terribly grim."

"It isn't, huh?" Bennion asked irritably. "I've already just missed getting my brains blown all over the street over nothing more than a horse."

"Maybe you were in the wrong. It wasn't your horse."

That was a fact which Bennion did not want to discuss, since it was true.

"I'll pay you," Gail said. "Consider this, if you, or anyone else, gets away with those bars, I'll file suit, and I'll be in the right, but that will result in delay, endless expense and trouble."

"It's a long jump from that glacier up there to a court. Where we sit right now, we're a hundred years away from what you're talking about."

Gail nodded. "That's why I want you on my side."

"You're not including Pancake?"

"All right, Pancake too."

"How much?"

"Five thousand each."

Bennion thought about it. "And if we don't accept, then you'll try down the street?"

He expected anger, but he saw fear and uncertainty instead. "I don't know what I'll do. I'm almost sorry that I came, at least, without help." Gail held that for a moment and then the anger did come. "No, I'm not sorry! I'm in the right."

"Sure you are," Bennion said tonelessly.

"Well?"

"I'll have to think it over."

"What is there to think over? The price?"

Bennion stalled. "Pancake won't say so, because he doesn't think the gold is there."

"I kept the figure low because I thought you'd be more likely to trust me." Gail's lips were stiff. "But that isn't the trouble, is it? The problem is that you don't trust me. You think I'll be making deals with everyone."

"That's the problem," Bennion said evenly. Her looks, her intelligence, her determination. She could mix her plays like a Split T quarterback, have every man in the basin, maybe even Pancake, running in all directions, each thinking that he had a special deal with her.

Without ever leaving the Nose Paint . . . She didn't look or act like the kind who would direct affairs into a bloody hassle.

Durwood did not look like a man who would do what he had done either.

Bennion tried to read her thoughts. Her attractiveness kept getting in his way. She was, he admitted, about as attractive as any chick he had ever seen and under different circumstances he would have been pitching for all he was worth.

He thought there was a line of desperation in her tone when she said, "I could say a straight split, with you and Pancake to settle with each other out of your half, but that wouldn't change your attitude, would it?"

"Are you making that offer?"

She hesitated. "No."

Bennion rose. "Maybe it would be better to find out if we're all chasing our tails, before we start dividing something that may not exist."

"It will be too late then, Johnny." She looked beaten, discouraged. Her face was pale. She sat at the table without moving as Bennion went to the door. "Would you mind going up to the glacier with me tomorrow?" It was like a child asking humbly for a favor.

Bennion hesitated. "Sure, I'll go up with you." He went out, dragging the door shut across the binding planks. He walked toward the freight yard, thinking, Am I a heel, or a smart character?

Pancake was in bed. His voice came muffled and grumpy from the wagon box, "Well, what kind of a proposition did she make?"

Bennion told him, and Pancake's comment was a disgusted grunt.

"Why do you think we can't trust her, Pancake?"

"Mainly because she's a woman. I could talk all night about the trouble women have given me, and then only be half started."

"She's a niece of Victor Shores."

"*Victor* Shores? Who the hell was he?" Pancake asked.

"A brother of Peyton, the Yankee general manager."

"That makes her a niece of Peyton's too, an' that's all to the worse. I never knowed anyone more worthless and downright no-good than that young whelp of a P. R. Shores, and that's a God's fact if there ever was one." Pancake rolled in his bed, bumping the side of the box and grunting. "Still, I guess you'd better help her, Johnny."

"That's a fast switch. Why?"

"Mainly because she's a woman."

SEVEN

From close against the icefall at the bottom of Hellsgrin the view was appalling and completely discouraged further exploration. The glacier came down in rounded spills like the dorsal part of some great monster humping its way over the rocks. Dark fragments of the mountain were coming to light again, glistening wetly in the clutch of the blue-white ice. Melting was faster around these rocks entrapped by Hellsgrin, so that they were set in little hollows like raisins punched into dough, not quite buried.

Hellsgrin ended in four major fingers separated by worn ridges of granite that still resisted the grinding action of the ice. Between the middle fingers the stream gushed forth, booming with a hollow sound that spoke of a gloomy passageway under the dying end of Hellsgrin.

Bennion saw Gail looking up the tumbled mass with an expression of awe. He touched her shoulder and pointed to the left, and she followed him up through the worn, slippery granite to get around the icefall.

The booming sound of the stream followed them and made talk impossible until they reached a point on the side of the mountain where the ice ran back in a hollow to form a wall that blocked off the noise of the glacier stream.

"Good grief!" Gail said, looking at what appeared to be an endless continuation of the icefall. "How did Stony Jackson ever do anything with that?"

"He went down that fall three times on ropes, and he actually took measurements and observations while he was doing it. Up higher, we can get around a little easier."

"That's where he used the ice shoes. I've seen them in the museum at Salida. I'm beginning to appreciate how remarkable that man really was."

They scrambled upward through the granite, swinging to the south with the curve of the glacier, and after a half hour more of hard climbing they were above the final plunge of Hellsgrin and could see ahead sharp *séracs* standing like vertical pennants.

The *séracs*, clustered thickly in the middle of the glacier, marked a point where an immovable ridge of granite under the ice forced the flow of the glacier upward. For two hundred yards beyond the wild field of frozen pennants the ice was gently sloping, and then it rose again, pinched in by the resisting shoulders of the granite, and then it ran on and on, curving sharply three times more in its deep channel until it reached its head under the Hellsgrin Trail.

That upper part of the glacier was not visible because of the wild ridges of rocks on both sides of Hellsgrin.

"How high have we climbed?" Gail asked.

"About fifteen hundred feet."

"I'll bet Durwood knows things about this glacier that we don't."

That was possible, Bennion thought, but there was no easy answer to Hellsgrin, and maybe no simple explanation of Durwood either. "Cold-blooded as an oyster," Pancake had said of Durwood that morning. "Along side that coarse-grained Tyner, he's a leopard compared to a pup."

"Well, he spoke up straight enough," Bennion said.

"Sure, where he had to tell the truth. He figured you'd been to that aereoplane. I like a good liar myself. You can catch him in time, but a man that tells the truth and lies in his thinking at the same time—there's a sonofabitch that's plumb dangerous."

Bennion said, "Did he say he'd walked in from Randall, and hurt his leg in a fall?"

"Naw! I guessed that. You see what I mean— he let me make a liar of myself. Them's the dangerous ones." With that, Pancake had taken a pick and shovel and gone over toward the Yankee Blade dump.

Whatever Durwood knew, or did not know, about the glacier, he was not rushing to look it over. Neither he nor Tyner had been up when Bennion and Gail left.

Gail pointed toward the *séracs*. "Somewhere near those teeth—would that be Point Seven, Jackson's area of major cracking and regelation?"

"That's it." Deep under the ice a stubborn ridge of granite barred the way, an unyielding barrier that was apparent by the buckling of the glacier at this point. Once the glacier crossed the buried ridge, that part of the ice moved with increasing speed, pulling away from the ice still jammed behind the barrier. Thus there was shearing that created crevasses which tapered down to darkness.

And then the moving pressure of the ice in the upper sections of the glacier would jam the cracks shut again and the ice would cement itself, until the breaks, occurred once more. It was an endless process of breaking and rejoining, part of the centimeter by centimeter crawling of the whole ice mass from Hellsgrin Trail to where the glacier ended on the mountain above Basin City.

Once in midsummer, near the spot where he was now standing, Bennion had heard the tight, frozen sound of shearing that seemed to run the full width of Hellsgrin, and it had been an eerie noise that chilled the deep, primitive responses in his being, and the hackles on his neck had tingled, as if he had heard the awful roar of some great beast from eons past.

"We can go out there, can't we?" Gail asked.

Bennion hesitated. "It's dangerous close to those crevasses, but if you want the full tour, let's go." He tossed her strips he had torn from a gunny sack. "Bind them as flat as you can on the bottoms of your shoes. They help quite a bit."

They left the rocks and went out slowly on the surface of the ice. The outer edge of the flow was only rippled but as they came closer to the center, climbing slightly toward the middle crest, they received the full effect of the wild field of *séracs* that stood like pointed tongues which had once cried out the agony of the ice as it broke and heaved to cross the deep hidden ridge.

Running everywhere through the frozen tongues were crevasses in a pattern of confusion. Gail edged close to one and peered down into the pale blue depths.

Bennion's toes dug tight against his boots. He wanted to reach out and draw her back. "Take it easy," he said.

"I won't fall in." She walked confidently along the jagged course of the crevasse, looking down into it, and then she came to the start of another crack running parallel with the first.

"Easy!" Bennion said, an edge of fear and irritation in his voice.

She walked ahead between the two crevasses and Bennion called again, "Damn it! Come back here. You make me nervous."

She turned to come back. Her left foot slipped and threw her off balance. It was not much, for she caught herself on one knee and was up again in an instant, but Bennion lived a long time during the instant.

He grabbed her by the wrist and dragged her back on the unbroken surface. "Now look, you're going to lose a guide if you do that again!"

"I guess you're right, but I really wasn't in any danger of falling in—until I slipped a little."

"Now you've seen Point Seven, so stay away from it."

She smiled at his irritation. "I didn't mean to give you a conniption fit."

"It always bothers me when other people, especially kids, go near a high place, or a deep place, or a flooding river."

"That's because you're naturally the fatherly type." Gail ignored Bennion's glare and began to study the rocks above the glacier. "Where're the pins that Jackson set in the rocks?"

He pointed. "If you keep looking you'll see one there. The other you can't see from here."

After a time she saw the piece of drill steel. "Ah, yes. Now where does the line cross?"

Bennion spread both arms. "This is roughly the angle, but the line is about thirty feet on up, above the first of the *séracs*."

"Yes, I can understand why Jackson didn't set the line below Point Seven."

That had been an unpleasant thought in Bennion's mind, too, the idea of what would happen to the body of a man crossing the continually breaking and rejamming area.

"Show me where the line actually runs," Gail said.

They walked on up the ice. "About here," Bennion said. "The first time I came, I made little rock monuments at the edge of the ice but they've been scoured away. We'd better sight in again and make some more markers."

They worked it out. Bennion went to the west side of the glacier and waited until Gail reached the pin on the east side. She waved him into line and he marked the spot at the edge of the ice, and then he had to climb to the steel pin on his side and sight her in line with the pins on the east side of the ice.

They built up monuments of rock, one on each side of the glacier and one in the middle.

For several moments Gail was motionless, studying the brief run of the gentle slope ahead, up to where the glacier rose steeply in another icefall. "Why a few days from now?" she said. "This ice moves by years and tenths of inches." She stepped a pace ahead. "Right here, right now."

Bennion smiled briefly, looking at the uneven, opaque surface. "If Jackson was exactly right, yes. He wasn't."

"Oh! Of course, you've looked before."

"Every summer for the last five years. I've shaved this ice in a hundred places to make little windows where I could look down. I've worn the knees out of my pants, huddling over those little peekholes. You don't see very far down into that ice, I'll tell you for sure. Sometimes there're layers of dust that absorb all the light. Sometimes the ice is so clear that the reflection beats back into your face and you can't see three feet deep.

"I've tried at night with lights. I've pitched a tent over the peekholes and tried in the daytime, experimenting to see what kind of light, and how much, gave the best penetration. Once I saw something about seven feet down and I spent the best part of two days picking ice. It was a rock."

Gail turned slowly, scanning the quarter mile width of the glacier. "You tried all the way across?"

"In spots, yes. I tried to work a pattern out. I've tried ahead of here too." Bennion's last statement was the most honest of all, although everything else he had said was also true. He thought of old Pancake's morning dissertation on the philosophy of truth and lies. Pancake would have said Bennion was using the Deadwood—the Durwood—method of telling the truth to confuse.

In Gail's expression he saw the same reaction

he had felt the first time he walked out on Hellsgrin at the place where Alonzo Pike was supposed to appear: Discouragement over the realization that the glacier was a mighty chunk of ice, that one could not walk upon it and see into it like looking into clear water, that Stony Jackson had set forth a terrific long-term guess, and that Hellsgrin just did not appear amenable to measurement, estimate or survey.

Distance put a beautiful shine on buried gold. It shone wondrously through ice that was not too thick and definitely not as rough as this surface. Bennion had been through the mill of easy believing and high hopes, until he tackled Hellsgrin on its own terms.

He watched Gail. She was deflated but she was not cast down into hopelessness. She said, "You tried all the way across, of course?"

Bennion nodded.

"It moves faster in the middle," she mused. "But how do we know where . . ." She shook her head. "There's even eddies higher up where the side channels have trouble making an even joining with the main mass."

"That's right, but of course the flow, over the long haul, is always down. It moves faster in constricted areas, faster in the summer, and then again, the entire movement is directly affected by snow conditions from year to year. I doubt that Stony Jackson was a climatologist, if fifty years can be considered a long enough period to even come under the head of climatology."

She gave him a rueful smile. "What are you trying to do—discourage me?"

"No, just giving you an idea of the situation."

"How did you make your windows in the ice?"

"I made a couple of ice planes, I suppose you'd call them. They look like long-handled hoes with the blades straightened out. They're over there in the rocks."

Gail said, "You've really given it the old college try. Be honest, Johnny, is it more because of your grandfather than the gold?"

"I don't know. Of course no one wants to think of an ancestor buried forever in a glacier, but if I find him, and the burro, and the gold, that proves him a thief."

Gail watched him keenly. "Some of the gold would alleviate the shock, wouldn't it? You said yourself that no one is responsible for his ancestors."

"I still feel the same way," Bennion said, "but I'm not thinking of the gold as all mine, like I used to."

"So?" Gail paused. "That means you're with me?"

"No, not yet." That sounded too blunt, so Bennion added, "If we want to be technical, you haven't proved that you really are the sole heir to the Yankee gold."

"I could, but . . ." Gail turned away from him. After a time, she said, "There's no doubt about those steel rods in the rocks?"

"They're the same pieces of drill steel Jackson himself put in fifty years ago. Where do you want to go now?"

"I'd like to see the whole glacier."

"It's a miserable haul through the rocks to get around to Hellsgrin Trail."

"I like miserable hauls, if there's something to see. Of course, if you want to go back and work on your fence . . ."

"Come on," Bennion said.

She did not follow him, however, but walked straight up the middle of the glacier to where the icefall rose in uneven corrugations. Bennion followed. One of the burlap strips around his boot was scuffed into a roll on the bottom, but he did not bother to adjust it.

They came to the face of the icefall jammed between massive shoulders of the gorge. By laborious measurement Bennion had established the fact that the fall was changed from Jackson's time. The profile was nearly the same, but sloughing of the granite shoulders had widened the restricted passage, so that the fall was wider now.

The most significant change was that it had receded about a hundred feet up the channel since the time Jackson had scrambled over the glacier in his fantastic ice shoes, swaying on the ends of ropes tied to drills sunk deep in the ice.

Gail leaned against the fall with both hands. "I think I could climb that."

"Don't try. It's almost vertical after you get above the first few humps."

"Some of the ice looks clear," Gail said, and began to climb.

She made it until her feet were higher than Bennion's head and there she stuck, flattened against the rolls. "I see what you mean," she said, looking above her. She put her face close to the ice to try to see into it.

Bennion saw her feet slip. He jumped to break her fall and the ridge of burlap on his foot caught against a half-buried stone. He fell hard on his knee and she came sliding past him on her stomach.

She tobogganed away for twenty feet, still on her stomach, before the friction of her clothing stopped her. She lay there laughing. Bennion slipped as he was getting up. He sat down with a jar. He stayed sitting, rubbing his knee, full of curses that he did not utter.

Gail was still laughing when she rose. "I guess you're right, as usual," and then she blinked when Bennion got up limping. "Did you twist something?"

"No damage that two weeks in traction won't cure." He hobbled toward the rocks, his knee feeling better as he went, and by the time he was off the ice, he was laughing.

They worked their way around through the rocks. They stood on the brim of a sheer cliff and saw below Jackson's Twist Devil at Point 4, a pothole in the ice where a stream swirled round and round, disappearing like water in a bathtub.

They fought their way around the deep and narrow side channels of Hellsgrin, looking down to where the sun never touched, far down where the snow was still winter white, where a subterranean wind was spinning powder on the uncompacted surface.

"You have to see it," Gail said. "The pictures and the drawings and the words don't mean much until you've been here."

When they broke out of the rocks to where they could look across the head of the glacier, they saw a man sitting on the trail above the bergschrund.

Tyner.

Bennion's whole mood changed in an instant. After Gail's fiasco on the icefall, the two of them had been more at ease, joking and laughing as they helped each other over the rocks. The sight of Tyner was a hard intrusion.

They climbed on up to the trail and went down to meet him. Tyner rose and tossed a cigarette off the trail and watched it roll toward the crevasse. He ignored Bennion. "Hi, doll baby," he said to

Gail. "I see you do your glaciering the hard way."

"If you want to see it, you've got to work a little."

Tyner grinned. "I don't detect any gold bars sticking out of your hip pocket."

It occurred to Bennion that Tyner might be considered a handsome man, if you took away the unmistakable whiskey flush showing under the skin around his cheekbones, and if you did not figure there was an insult just behind his grin. The grizzled mustache gave him a halfway distinguished look, when his mouth was still.

"The way to get a good look at this glacier—" Tyner said, and then he swooped Gail up and stepped to the edge of the trail with her in his arms. He moved with an easy strength and lightness that surprised Bennion.

Tyner held her over the edge of the drop, laughing. "How about it? The next time I offer you a drink, are you going to turn me down?"

"Cut it out!" Gail said, and Bennion saw the terror in her eyes. "I'll drink the whole bottle the next time."

Tyner laughed and swung her back to her feet on the trail. "You make a nice armful, doll baby. I'm going to hold you to that promise." He patted her lightly on the rear when she turned to get against the cliff.

The whole thing had caught Bennion flat-footed. Most of all it was Tyner's idiotic act of holding Gail above the rocks and snow that sloped straight down to the crevasse that caused the boiling inside Bennion.

But this was no place to brawl. Tyner watched his reaction, then grinned and turned to Gail, "Going down, madam?"

They started down the trail, Bennion in the rear. Tyner kept talking to Gail, laughing at his own remarks, undisturbed by her silence. They came around the shoulder of the mountain to where the fall was less steep, where the trail was wider for a few feet.

Tyner said, "Your backfield's in motion, Gail," and patted her again.

"Wait a minute, Gail," Bennion said. "Switch places with me."

Tyner stopped and turned. "Never mind, cowboy, she's doing all right where—"

Bennion shouldered him hard. He knocked Tyner down at the edge of the trail. Bennion scooped up a rock the size of a beer can. He stood ready to smash it into Tyner's face if the man came at him. Tyner started to surge up and then the motion slowed and stopped as he stared at Bennion's face.

The drive went out of Tyner. His lips fell from tightness back to looseness and the sparks in his eyes faded to dullness. He stood up slowly with his arms at his sides, the coward that Pancake said he was.

The change in him killed Bennion's anger. He did not look at Tyner as he walked past him and on past Gail, and they all went down the mountain in silence.

EIGHT

West of the caved portal of the Yankee Blade tunnel, the mountain ran up wildly in deep scored channels that carried leaping waterfalls when the snow was melting. Up there on one of the spines that divided two plunging crevices a rusted piece of iron pipe, still held by its steel pegs, marked the last of the waterline that had run from a high spring to the house of the general manager of the Yankee Blade Company.

The house itself was long since gone, burned by some careless person who had camped out in it after Basin City declined to nothing. Brown-tone pictures showed it as a white, two-storied house replete with gingerbread along all overhangs and cornered on the upper story with atrocious round tower rooms enclosed by curving glass.

It had stood just east of the Yankee Blade tunnel on a relatively level piece of ground that commanded a good view of the shacks along the river below the Yankee dump.

George Durwood was poking among the ruins. Now and then he turned over with the side of his foot lumps of fire-fused glass and other artifacts. Limping slightly, he picked his way through the ruins, his eyes sharp with thought, and then he sat on the foundation, surveying the position of the rock-walled safe room of the mill in relation to the town, the mill itself, and Hellsgrin Trail.

He made what he could of that, and then he climbed the reddish dump of the Yankee tunnel and went over to the collapsed portal. He studied it as if it held something worth observing, dry rotted timbers sticking out of the mass of rock and wash, the clear stream running from beneath the spill, running beside rotted ties and rusting rails that reached a mile back into the mountain.

Durwood went on past the blacksmith shop and dryroom, to the edge of the dump. He looked down to where Pancake was digging a trench in loose ground at the bottom of one of the ravinelike creases in the mountain. The black dog that belonged to the woman was lying on the bank.

Pancake paused in his digging to speak to the dog, "You're a fake, Saber. First, you want to tear me apart, then you take up with Sam Harding, and now you want to make friends with me. A fake is all you are."

The dog wagged its tail a little, as if to say that it was satisfied with things at present but would wait a little longer before allowing the relationship to ripen.

Unobserved so far, Durwood stayed where he was. What was Whiskers up to anyway? His eyes followed the crease up the grim, plunging slope

120

to where it began near the glory hole where the first prospecting had revealed the riches of the Yankee Blade. In a few places up there, stark gray timbers marked the line of the tram the first company had built to work the mine.

What was old Whiskers trying to prove? Durwood called down, "Any pay dirt, pardner?"

Saber leaped up with a growl. Pancake swung around, his forehead shining with sweat. "Oh, it's Deadwood. Shut up, Saber, it's all right."

Durwood worked his way down the slope of the dump. It tickled him the way the old man miscalled his name. He sat down on a rock and studied the trench. Pancake had moved several yards of dirt since morning, even if it was nothing more than loose wash.

Never call a man crazy, Durwood thought, until you knew what he was doing; and old Pancake was far from crazy.

"Something the old-timers overlooked?" Durwood asked.

Pancake put one foot up on the side of the trench. "They didn't find all the gold in the mountains."

"Isn't that a funny place for it?"

"Yep!" Pancake pointed up the mountain. "It was a funny place up there too, that whole patch of mountain that's all caved in now. It's where you happen to find it, Deadwood."

Durwood smiled. "I go for that. What were the

timbers doing up there, that broken line you can see?"

"That? That was the old double-track tram the first company tried to operate with." Pancake pulled a cigar from his pocket and lit it. He sat down on the edge of the trench. "Fall of 1900, I think it was, the Yankee was staked. This Joe McGee layout was going to mine right from the surface, right up there."

"You were here?" Durwood asked.

"I was around. No roads in here or nothing, not even a trail then. This outfit brought in everything by mule, a steam hoist knocked down in pieces, a little old boiler and that was in pieces too. They come in across the Granites by way of where Bennion's ranch is now, and—"

"That's the best way?" Durwood asked. "Could you get a jeep through there now?"

Pancake scowled. "I doubt it. You want to hear what I was trying to say, or not."

"Sorry." Durwood flipped a small rock from his thumb toward the gaping pocket of Pancake's coat lying on a rock. The rock hit the cloth and slid into the pocket.

"They brought four, five boilermakers clean from some engine company in Pittsburgh. Paid 'em fearful wages. Two of 'em damn near died of fright riding mules in here to put that boiler together. Of course they couldn't do much good boilermaking here with sheets that was some bent up and flues that was screwgeed from being whacked agin rocks and trees when the mules was packing them in. Besides, them boilermakers was afraid of bears and Indians.

"They put her together but there was missing rivets and stuff like that and she jetted steam like a secondhand calliope. Under the conditions I guess the boilermakers done as well as could be expected. Meantime the company was building the double-track tram up to the discovery hole. You can see a little of the dump up there yet. It was a steep lash-up, if ever there was one. Gravity. The cable went around a big shiv wheel at the top.

"The loaded car coming down was supposed to pull two empty cars going up. She was too steep of course to run that simple, and that's where the hoist come in down here on the crick. The cable from it was tailed into the last empty so the engineer could brake the whole shebang. Only trouble was—the track was too steep, the loaded car too heavy, the brake on the hoist too little, and the boiler too leaky.

"It took two men running back and forth to the creek with buckets to pour enough water into the boiler so she wouldn't blow up. When they got a little too much water, the steam pressure dropped and the engineer had to hold with nothing but his mechanical brakes. But most of the time there wasn't enough water. About that time, let one of those men stumble a little and the engineer raised out of his seat, ready to jump and run for it.

"That engineer needed six eyes, one to watch the water gauge, one for the steam gauge, one to see that the water carriers were still hustling, one to watch the loaded car coming straight at him off the mountain, one to see if his cable was fouling up in the track, and another to see if his brakes were burning.

"One day the water hustlers worked harder than usual. New men on the job. The engineer didn't have enough steam to pull back with and his brakes began to go. That loaded car was picking up speed. When he seen she was going, he sailed off the seat and lit running. The car wasn't too far up the mountain that time—just far enough to knock pieces of the hoist halfway across the basin when she hit."

Pancake paused to get his cigar going again. "Well, they mule-packed another hoist and started again. The next time things come loose it was a hell-busting mess. Both empties going up was loaded with men, four in a car, and one car had a lot of long drill steel in it. The cars were just about at the passing point when the cable snapped and come lashing down the hill like a crazy snake. Two men jumped as quick as they seen what happened.

"One of them got killed, but the other got out

of it with just a busted leg. The other five didn't get out until the empties derailed, sliding and smashing over the rocks. That long steel in the one car acted like an egg beater when the ends of it, sticking up above the box, started hitting rocks. It chopped two of those miners into pieces, and of course the other four was killed too."

Durwood had been grinning at parts of the story. Now he looked up the savage heights and began to laugh. He went on laughing until his cheeks were wet and he had to take a deep, dragging breath. "Like an egg beater!" he gasped, and then he laughed again while Pancake watched him uneasily.

After Durwood got control of himself, Pancake went on slowly. "That wound up the first outfit. The company Shores managed bought 'em out and started tunneling from down here to get under the ore, which was the proper way." Pancake stood up suddenly and began digging again.

"That was some story, old-timer." Durwood flipped another rock; he had been flipping them all the time Pancake was talking. "What did you do around here in 1909?"

"Dealt cards," Pancake answered curtly.

"You knew Shores, huh, and all the others?"

"Yeah."

Durwood got up. "Well, cut me in when you strike it rich. We'll build another tram." He laughed. "I'm going back and doctor my knee.

Stop by and have a drink of Tyner's whiskey with me. He's got enough to restock the saloon."

"Thanks. I don't use it." Pancake went on shoveling.

He worked only until Durwood was gone and then he climbed from the shallow trench as if he had turned his last shovelful of dirt for all time. He watched Durwood cross the creek and go to his cabin.

Sonofabitch, that Durwood was a bad oyster for sure.

Pancake put on his coat. After a few moments the weight of it made him frown and then he discovered that one pocket was full of small rocks. Oh, maybe that was why Durwood had laughed so hard.

Over a childish stunt like that? No . . . no, it wasn't the reason. He had been only politely interested in the story most of the time, smiling a little when Pancake was telling about the men scooting to the creek with buckets and the hoist engineer trying to roll his eyes in six places at one time.

The part that had given him the laughing fit was those two cars with men in them breaking loose on the mountain. Jesus Christ, what kind of man was this grandson of old Jackson's? A man could bust himself laughing at some pretty rough deals, even death, which sometimes had its funny aspects; but Durwood's laughter had been obscene and shocking, like he wasn't no part of the human race.

Pancake looked at the trench. Maybe he wouldn't dig another inch there. He stared across the creek, remembering a different view than the forlorn ruins he now saw. He remembered strength and youngness and the will to do anything that struck his fancy, and he remembered some of the great errors he had committed and trusting people he had wronged.

There was Alice, for one. She floated in his vision for a moment, gentle, believing, trusting him.

It was like reaching the end of a long trail and looking back, knowing that much had to be forgotten because remembering did no good. But never, never in his life, had he derived Satanic pleasure at the thought of death or human suffering.

Jesus, that Durwood . . .

Time caught up with Pancake, the time that he had always laughed at and defied. He did not feel old, it was not that at all, although he knew that others considered him a relic; instead, he felt the weight of guilt, as a man who wakens in the night for no reason and recalls his long-ago acts of cowardice and passion and violence and weakness and the things that were mean and little and never should have been.

He looked at the trench and shook his head.

How could Durwood's laughter do this to him, even though it was a roaring from some deep darkness in the man's spirit, from something that belonged back in the days when Hellsgrin filled this whole basin and life of any kind had no dignity.

Pancake was shaken and he could not deny it, but he was an old man of tough spirit who had lived too long and seen too much to be jarred out of his boots completely by the cold depravity of Durwood, or any other human being. He dumped the rocks out of his pocket and tramped toward town. It was time to eat dinner anyway. To hell with Durwood; he could be handled. Youth and cold-bloodedness and toughness did not necessarily make any man invincible.

Over near the fenced pasture he saw Saber visiting Sam Harding, both the dog and the burro getting the smells and intentions of each other. That was one thing about animals, they were incapable of laughing at each other's misfortunes.

After Pancake crossed the stream near the jackstraw of timbers and gray boards that had once been the Yankee mill, he heard the tinkle of rocks on Hellsgrin Trail and looked up to see three people coming down. They were not talking and they were striding along as if they had serious business.

Johnny, the Gail girl, and Tyner.

Saber came thumping up the meadow. He

stopped to throw water off his coat and then he walked in and muzzled Pancake's hand. Pancake grinned. "You damned old black cuss. I don't want anything to do with you, you hear me?" He patted the dog's head. "Get over there and see your mistress, you man-eater."

At the upper end of the mill Tyner left the other two and went toward the burned house, but it was obvious that he had no real purpose there because he turned and stood watching Bennion and the woman. They started talking soon after they separated from Tyner, and that was when Saber went splashing across the creek to greet Gail.

Pancake could not hear what they were saying, but the sound of their voices reassured him. By God, the Durwoods of the world were greatly outnumbered by the Bennions. A man who was somewhere in between the two generally threw his weight in with the Bennions.

He saw Gail and Johnny heading toward the old safe room.

Once more Pancake got his cigar to going, and then he flourished it in his hand as he went toward camp, singing.

"A Spanish cavalier stood in his retreat,
And in his retreat sang a song, dear.
The music so sweet I ofttimes repeat.
Remember what I say and be true, dear . . ."

Gail stopped when she heard the burst of singing, standing for a moment watching Pancake going toward the freight yard. "That's an oldie."

"My father used to sing it all the time," Bennion said. "You want to hear the rest of it?" He took a deep breath.

"Never mind, not that I doubt your vocal prowess." Saber came charging up, and Gail said, "Avast there, you wetback."

The safe lay on its side, its door battered and chisel-marked, but still locked. Back of it were the ruins of the masonry wall where it had been embedded.

"You mean that thing hasn't been open since—" Gail said.

"No!" Bennion laughed. "It was left standing open when the mine was shut down, so no one would damage it, but some smart character closed it and turned the knob. After that everyone who came along had to take a crack at it. There's nothing like a locked door to challenge vandals. That's why I don't have a lock on anything in Basin City."

Gail knelt and turned the dial. "Why, that would still work!"

"I suppose so. There was a heavy log roof on this place until a few years ago when it finally rotted through."

A rat popped out of the broken wall behind the safe. It sat there boldly a few feet away. Saber stiffened, trembling, until Gail said, "Get him, Saber, if you think you can."

Saber could not, but he had a fine, snuffling time of pawing rocks and throwing dust.

Gail climbed over the wreckage to the back of the safe. "I see." The back end of the safe, concrete between metal walls, had been blasted open. "Somebody had to look, didn't they?"

"They always do. That's the way it was the first time I ever saw it."

They went on toward town. "Do you have any pictures of your grandfather?" Gail asked.

"Some," Bennion said. A wedding picture that made his hair and mustache look black, instead of sandy. A picture of him taken beside the Yankee mill, standing with the big wheels of the company, all of them dressed in rubber boots and slickers, as if they had just come from a tour of the mine. "Why?"

"I just wondered. How tall was he?"

"Five, nine, at a guess. My mother once told me he was as tall as Stony Jackson and she believed it, but in the picture I have of him, taken here at the mill in 1905, he was standing two people away from Jackson and he was at least six inches shorter. We know Jackson was six feet, three."

"How do you know?"

"The average height of men was inches shorter fifty years ago than it is now, so a tall man always drew comment. *The Crusher*, the old

Smelter Town paper, mentioned several times that Jackson was a towering man."

"I've read *The Crusher*," Gail said. "But 'towering' isn't very accurate."

"I remember something better. Jackson himself, in a *Century Magazine* story about Hellsgrin wrote something like this, 'a big-footed, scared man lowering himself down an icefall on a rope that was too short, with every inch of his six foot, three frame stretching to make up for the shortcomings of the rope.' Remember that?"

"Hmn," Gail said, giving Bennion a searching look. "That's one I missed. You certainly soaked up everything there is about Jackson, it seems."

"I've never seen his personal letters."

"All right," Gail said, "so your grandfather was five, nine. What color eyes, hair, so forth?"

"Sandy hair. I don't know about his eyes. Fair complexion. Pretty good features, from the little you can tell from those old pictures. Weighed about a hundred and fifty, I'd guess." Once more Bennion asked, "Why?"

"Oh, I just wondered if he looked like you."

They stopped at the camp in the freight yard. Pancake was on his knees, fanning the fire with his hat. "Well," he said, "I suppose you got wet up there on the ice."

"I broke all my fingernails on one deal, I'll tell you that," Gail said. "How about you and Johnny coming over for dinner this evening. I've got two canned chickens."

"You mean supper?" Pancake said. "I'm just before wrastling up dinner right now. Canned chicken, by Ned!"

"The virtue of having a stink wagon to haul the chow," Gail said.

"You can't insult me with chicken," Pancake said. "Me and Johnny will be there."

Bennion nodded. "Sure. It's one o'clock now. As soon as we have dinner we can come over and start waiting for your dinner."

"That's fine with me." Gail gave him an amused, speculative smile. "I've got something that will interest you."

"You sure have," Bennion said.

"On the level, I've got an item. The 1909 files of the *Basin Advocate*."

"No kidding!" Bennion said. "I've tried for years to find those, but there isn't supposed to be a file in existence. Where—"

"It's a long story." Gail started away. "Six o'clock? Come over earlier if you want to read."

After she was gone, Bennion studied Pancake. "You're really eighty-two, Pancake?"

"I am."

"What color was your hair?"

Pancake rose from his knees without a lurch or grunt to indicate stiffness. "Light brown, or something. It's been so long ago, I don't rightly remember. Always had a lot of it."

His eyes were brown. He was maybe five feet, eight inches tall. Except for a good forehead, his features were lost behind the white beard. "That's no way to talk to a decent woman, boy."

"What do you mean?"

"She said she had something to interest you, and you made that smart-alec crack about she sure did." Pancake shook his head. "What kind of loose talk is that?" He was dead serious.

Like a father reproving a son.

NINE

After he ate, Bennion went to see about the horses. On his way he caught a glimpse of Tyner doing the cooking and Durwood lying on a bunk in the cabin. For some reason old Pancake was good and shook-up about Durwood, almost as if he was afraid of the man, but he had not said why.

Bennion's horses and Tyner's were visiting across the pasture fence. Sam Harding was foraging near the creek and there close to him was Saber, rolling on his back in the grass, as if to prove to the burro that he was a friendly fellow who knew a few tricks.

Tyner's packhorse seemed to be a trifle better. Bennion led him by the mane, watching him walk. Yes, he was getting along all right, but he would not be able to carry a pack for another week, at least. Once more Bennion took the animal down to the creek and made him stand with his forefeet in the icy stream.

Three huge B-52's came over the basin. Bennion saw their con trails before he heard any noise and then he watched the white vapor tail out long across the sky and suddenly the sound of the jets rocked down into the basin with heavy thunder. He watched until the bombers were specks on the western horizon, and by then the first swift, clean marks of their con trails were growing fluffy and shapeless and blowing away eight thousand feet above.

Three swept wing planes. Thirty million dollars. The easy sweep of the bombers emphasized the hard remoteness of the basin, its position lost in time. Bennion kept staring at the sky until all the sound was gone, and then the old uneasiness returned.

He saw Gail cross the street with a water bucket, and not long afterward she and Pancake returned, with Pancake carrying the water. He went inside the Nose Paint with her.

Why was he digging over there against the mountain? All he had said was, "I don't know what I'm doing, but we'll find out. We'll find out. It won't be the first hole I've dug on speculation."

As Bennion went up the street he saw Pancake headed back to camp.

Gail was scrubbing the saloon floor with a gunny sack wired to the end of a splintery mop handle. "You're ruining the dump," Bennion said. "Pancake and I will never feel at home in here after this."

"Don't worry. It won't last that long. I could use two more buckets of water."

"Civilization rides again in Basin City," Bennion said, and went to carry water. He helped finish the job. The place did look a little better, he admitted.

Gail said, "You could start an antique shop with that stuff along the wall."

"Yeah. An elk hunter named Wingate mentioned that once and gave me such a pitch that I've hated everyone since who mentioned the subject. I did consider packing some of that stuff out, but I decided it wouldn't be in very good condition by the time it reached Randall."

"No problem," Gail said. "Wait until someone dozes a road down from that aquamarine mine and people will carry everything away for you, for free. Sit down. I'll get the newspaper file."

They sat at the poker table. The *Basin Advocate* was a weekly, small format, four pages, surprisingly little of the print boilerplate. "I've known for a long time where the complete files were," Gail said. "In the estate of one of the former Yankee stockholders, but it wasn't until the week before I left San Francisco that the estate was finally settled and I could buy the files."

"You've read this one?"

"Skipped through. I intended to read them thoroughly on the way here, but after I was sort of upset in Salt Lake . . . Well, I didn't take the time."

"What about the guy who was going to come with you?"

Gail's expression was reserved. "What about him?"

"Did he have any bearing on the background of Basin City, or any particular knowledge of—"

"No, no! Just a man I knew. He thought I was a little crazy for carrying through and maybe I thought he was a bit gutless for backing out. That's all over now."

Bennion said, "He might have been right." He started to open the file and then closed it. "I think we'd better start burning bridges."

"What do you mean?"

"The first thing—bust the spark plugs in your jeep engine. I don't mean take them out, I mean smash them up so there's no question or reservation about it."

The woman took her time with that before she asked, "What about the horses?"

"I'll take care of them."

"Turn them loose?"

"Mine are already loose," Bennion said. "Turning Tyner's loose will work, with the saddle horse, at least. Mine will take a little more doing."

Gail studied him quietly. Behind her calmness, fear was showing, not panicky fright but a solid appreciation of the implications in Bennion's plan. "What about Sam Harding?" she asked.

"Yeah, the burro is a problem that's been worrying me some. I'll talk to Pancake about Sam Harding."

"This bridge burning," Gail said, "does that mean that you and I and Pancake are allies?"

Bennion nodded.

"And you accept my offer?"

"Let's work that out later." Bennion opened the newspaper file and turned to the issue following the robbery of the Yankee Blade mill. The one-column headlines were small, the content of the first story remarkably restrained. Alonzo Pike was missing and so was an undetermined number of golden bars from the mill strong room, but Gen'l Mgr. P. R. Shores was not yet ready to make a categorical statement concerning the affair.

Bennion and Gail sat close together as they read the follow-up stories. The third week after the robbery, coverage was greater, for by then Shores announced that ninety thousand dollars was missing, and made his reluctant, if somewhat belated, statement that Pike must be guilty, and said that detectives were working on the case.

By June the story was fading. It flared up in late summer when Jackson made his prediction, but the editor did not take kindly to Jackson's long-range guess, pointing out acidly that Jackson was the same engineer who was also saying that the Yankee Blade was about worked out, when anyone with common sense knew that the Yankee was good for another thirty years of heavy production.

After that there was an occasional single paragraph of rumor about Pike's whereabouts, with sharp editorial comment on the inability of Pinkerton men to do much more than chase women and run up large expense accounts.

All the stories put together revealed nothing essential that Bennion did not know already. Only one unimportant fact drew comment from him: ". . . Victor Shores, reported to be one of the heavy investors of the Yankee Company, arrived in our city today on the morning stage, to take personal charge of the investigation. . . ."

That was three days after the robbery.

"Where did Victor Shores live?" he asked Gail.

"Waverly, Iowa."

"And three days later he got here, in the morning?"

"He was on his way," Gail said. "He always came out every summer. He didn't know about the robbery until he reached Smelter Town."

"April isn't summer in this basin. Was that his usual time for coming out—April?"

"I have no idea. Maybe he came earlier for some reason." Gail turned the pages, searching the faded print for further information about the robbery. For just an instant something in her manner caused Bennion doubt, as if she had smoothly sheered away from something she did not wish to talk about.

He forgot it a moment later when she put her

finger on a paragraph and said, "Look there."

It was a short item. "There are no new developments this week from the fracas L. G. Riddle, the irascible swamper of the Nose Paint, had recently with members of the Golden Eagles when they turned down his application to join their estimable organization. Mr. Riddle swears that if Boiler Manor ever catches fire and he does not get satisfactory service, he will sue everyone in Basin City to the hilt. His very words, to the hilt."

Gail said, "That's Pancake. What's a swamper?"

"In this case, a fellow that cleans up saloons." It was natural enough, Bennion thought. Old Pancake, with all his hot air, would not admit to having been a swamper when he could assume the higher status of a gambler.

"What was Boiler Manor?" Gail asked. "Some more of that editor's quaint humor?"

Bennion shrugged. The file had been disappointing, but old documents were generally ninety-eight per cent that way when you wanted specific information. He rose from the table restlessly, once more taken with the futility of trying to reconstruct the past. The answer he wanted was in Hellsgrin, now, or it was not anywhere to be known.

"Does anyone else but me know you have that gun?" he asked.

Gail shook her head.

"Keep it that way."

"Maybe you're worrying about trouble that won't be." Gail was more hopeful than believing.

"If the gold shows up, I know we're in for trouble. If it doesn't, all I've got is a minor argument over a horse to settle with Tyner." Bennion shook his head. "We've got to figure the worst and get set for it now, and hope it never happens."

"I know that's logical, but—"

"More people walked in and out of here than ever rode," Bennion said, "but I never heard of anyone doing it with three hundred pounds on his back."

"I get the point," Gail said, still not happy with the plan. "Oh, by the way, Pancake just told me that Durwood didn't have a gun when he stopped Tyner from shooting you. Pancake was off to the side where he could see into the cabin. He said Durwood just sat on his bunk and ordered Tyner to lower the rifle." She paused. "Pancake seems to be afraid of Durwood. Why?"

"I don't know." Bennion went out to find Pancake. He saw the old man going toward his diggings, skirting the swamp near the creek. Durwood and Tyner were sitting on the step in front of their quarters.

As Bennion passed, Tyner said, "Which horse are you figuring on crippling now, doctor?"

Bennion ignored him. Durwood shook his head slightly and smiled patiently, conveying the impression that he too had about enough of Tyner, but that they had to put up with him the best way they could.

As soon as Bennion had done something about the horses, his motive would be clear, but he doubted that Durwood would throw a fit over a fact accomplished, as Tyner undoubtedly would; but Bennion was not going to be able to do anything with the two of them standing by. He examined the packhorse again and then went over to see Pancake.

Pancake was cleaning out a former excavation; that was obvious because of the rock walls. He was on rock bottom at one end and it appeared that he intended to go all the way.

"What was it, Pancake?"

"Oh, that damn fool Shores had this trenched to see if he could pick up a vein. Wasn't no real veins in this whole country, to start with. Sure, there was some good ore all along here, but anybody knowed it was washed from clean up there where the big funnel cropped out on the surface."

"I see. You think the gold bars are there?"

"Hell no!" Pancake snorted. "I'll let you know what I think is here when I find it, if I do."

"I see you and the dog are getting along."

Pancake looked at Saber, lying on the cool dirt below the trench. "Bothers the life out of me, but I have to put up with him, I guess."

"Pancake, would Sam Harding come back if I took him away, say four or five miles?"

"Most likely." Pancake leaned on his shovel, staring at Bennion, and he had no difficulty following Bennion's thoughts. "Try it. You can try it, Johnny."

"The trouble is, I can't take the chance until night, or unless they . . ." And then Bennion saw Tyner and Durwood going toward the glacier. Once they got above the great cliff fall at the lower end . . . They were taking their time and Durwood was favoring one leg, but they were tackling the rocky outfall and making steady progress.

"Pancake, did you ever try to get in the Golden Eagles, the fire company Shores organized?"

The old man gave Bennion a startled look, and then he sat down on the edge of the trench and stared at his feet. "Yes, I did."

"What was Boiler Manor?"

Pancake looked up with a hangdog expression and then lowered his gaze. "It was a shack laid up against the side of an old boiler foundation there by the crick. Who told you about that?"

"Gail and I read it in the *Basin Advocate*."

"Yeah, I remember." Pancake flared up. "That goddamn' editor! He was a no-good drunkard! Sure, maybe I wasn't as high-toned as those nabobs in the Eagles, them and their tall hats and all. I swamped in the saloon that winter until I

144

could get out and go prospecting. Nobody ever had to grubstake me. What I did I did myself, and when I hit it rich, there was nobody to come back on me and say they owned half of what I made. There wasn't no shame in—"

"Who said there was? You don't have to convince me, Pancake." Bennion kept one eye on the two men going toward Hellsgrin.

"Well you're the one that tried to make some crime out of it!" Pancake said testily. "Why, let me tell you something, the very first time I struck it, out in Nevada, I could've bought and sold that editor and that crooked P. R. Shores too. I'll say this for Shores, though; it wasn't so much him that kept me out of the Eagles as it was some of them others. The idea of a saloon swamper wearing that gaudy uniform and hobnobbing with gentlemen sort of tickled Shores, but—"

"Forget it, Pancake. I didn't mean to stir up an international incident."

"Why the hell did you start then?"

To change the subject, Bennion said, "You must have known Victor Shores, the brother. The paper said he was here a few days after the robbery."

"Oh yeah, him. The other day I didn't want to talk about him. I remember him all right. He was a real puss-in-the-boots, that Victor. He wouldn't have said 'manure' if he'd fallen in a barnyard full of it. Fussy, dressy, always catching a cold. Whiskey was a sin to him and his kind. He used to come here in the summer and prod and poke around the Yankee and give P. R. fits." Pancake paused for breath. "About that swamping job I took—"

"I'll see you later, Pancake."

The old man was still grumbling when Bennion hurried away.

After Tyner and Durwood were out of sight, Bennion waited another ten minutes. Then he turned Tyner's horses out of the pasture and started them down the creek. The packhorse was limping, but the urge to go home was just as strong in him as in the saddle horse, since both of them had been rental animals most of their lives.

Bennion rode Stranger bareback, with Sam Harding in tow, and Frog following readily. The bad place on the trail was where it went in close under the dark rocks at the edge of the glacier. Bennion kept looking up to see if Tyner and Durwood were waiting there.

His back itched until he was clear of that exposure and over the first break and by then high rock ridges separated him from the ice canyons of Hellsgrin. He stopped and looked down on Basin City.

Gail was at her jeep and the hood was up. Pancake was a tiny figure scratching away in his trench. Tyner's horses were far down the old road, going slower now, foraging a little, but still moving toward home. They would never go into the canyon; they would find a route of their own through the mountains.

It would take them a long time to reach the Bonnet, and when they wandered in, Sandy Mulford would think no more about it than to comment profanely on the fact that another greenhorn had let his animals get away. Mulford would wait four or five days for Tyner to come limping in before he did anything about looking for him.

Gail put the hood down and went back into the Nose Paint.

Bennion went three miles farther before he decided it was far enough, and that bareback riding was now a bit different from when he was a kid. He took the rope off Sam Harding and said, "Beat it!"

Sam Harding gave him a thoughtful look and stood still.

Stranger and Frog leaped out with startled grunts when Bennion whacked them with the rope, but they did not go far before they stopped and looked back at him. "Go on, get out of here!"

The horses began to eat. Sam Harding remained standing in brooding silence. Bennion drove his horses another hundred yards toward home and then he turned back. It was hard to say. They might come back to Basin City. If they went home, it was unlikely that they would set a beeline, because the grass was good and for all

147

they knew they had been turned out to pasture.

They watched Bennion walk away. Sam Harding did not bother to do that; he stood like a rock, thinking his mysterious burro thoughts.

As Bennion went down the trail past the glacier he saw no tracks indicating that Tyner and Durwood had returned to Basin City. Tyner's horses were gone now. Bennion kept looking down the road, and up toward Volcano Pass, and at the bare slope where Gail had pioneered a jeep trail. Once he had worried greatly about the number of people who might come to the basin.

Now he knew it would be better if more people, a great many people, would suddenly descend on the ghost town.

He could not see Pancake. The door of the Nose Paint was closed. Saber was nowhere in sight. Bennion found himself going down the steep trail at a trot. He hammered on the saloon door and waited only an instant before plunging in. Gail was not there.

Damn, the place was quiet. It always was, but now it was deathly quiet. Bennion went back to the street, and it was then that Gail came around the corner of the building with her hands full of sun-purpled bottles, with Saber trailing behind her.

Bennion tried not to show his relief. "Where's Pancake?"

"Taking a nap."

He glanced toward the glacier. "They're still up there?"

"I've been watching. They haven't come back."

Bennion looked at the bottles. "What are you going to do with those?"

"I collect purple bottles." Gail spoke as if everything were normal, as if she had nothing more to do than kick around in tin-can piles. And then she said, "I broke up things in the jeep. I had to force myself to do it. You think it was the right move—everything we did?"

"Yes," Bennion said, and hoped it was right.

TEN

The dinner was a pleasant, although temporary, insulation against worries. Perhaps fortified by his afternoon nap, Pancake was in fine form, discoursing upon his adventures in South American mining. Real or fancied; one could not tell, but if Pancake had not been in Peru, he most certainly had listened well to someone who had been there.

The chicken was demolished and they were having coffee. Pancake paused to blow an expensive cloud of cigar smoke toward the ceiling. "I had these hundred Peruvian miners. About fifty cents a day, American. They could tote more on their back in a basket than—"

A burro brayed in the street. Sam Harding was back and he wanted everyone to know it.

"He didn't take long," Bennion said. It was not yet dusk.

"Don't worry," Pancake said. "Nobody is going to pack anything on him but me—if there was anything to pack. He just won't work for strangers."

Saber whined and went to the door. Gail let the dog out and watched a few moments as he paced off down the street with the burro.

"Now about this mining deal in Chile—" Pancake said.

"Peru," Gail corrected.

"Peru, Colombia, Chile, clean down to Tierra del Fuego," Pancake said. "I even seen a glacier at Fuego, the Romance, or some such. It sprawls off the cliff with its paws in the water like nothing you ever seen."

"La Romanche," Gail said. "Did you really—"

Tyner and Durwood walked in suddenly. "We were beginning to feel like outcasts," Durwood said. He pulled a chair away from the wall and carried it down to the table. Tyner remained standing, looking at the furniture along the wall.

Gail glanced at Bennion quickly. Then she offered the visitors coffee. Tyner shook his head. Durwood said, "Thank you. I've been drinking Tyner's corrosive sublimate."

"It suits me," Tyner growled.

Pancake seemed to have shrunk. He was staring at Durwood with a strange expression, as if the man terrified him.

Whatever it was, Bennion could not see it in Durwood's face. The man was assured and pleasant, and all his expressions seemed to come cleanly from his thinking, with his features masking nothing.

"We aren't cooperating very well, for natural reasons, I suppose." Durwood tried the coffee and nodded approval. "I think we ought to be able to

151

trust each other better, and that's my reason for intruding."

"What do you call cooperation?" Bennion asked.

"Just being honest with each other. We're not doing that, you know. We're here for the same purpose. We all know it and admit it, and yet we're trying to out-maneuver each other before we have anything concrete to struggle over." Durwood smiled around the table.

"What's your proposal?" Bennion asked.

"Nothing but common sense." Durwood frowned in the manner of one getting ready to make a point so thoroughly and honestly that it could not be disputed. "We have the possibility of a large amount of gold reaching a certain point in a glacier, somewhere near a certain time. I don't go overboard on my grandfather's theories, by any means. Until something happens, why are we fighting?"

"And when it happens?" Bennion asked.

Durwood raised his brows. He looked like a man who has been asked a question with an obvious answer, and a man with patience to give the answer. "Why," he said, "I think we're all civilized people who can work out satisfactory solutions to our problems. The point is we have no problem yet."

"If there's gold from the Yankee Blade mill in Hellsgrin, it's mine by legal right," Gail said.

"What kind of problem would that bring up, as far as you're concerned?"

"The problem of proving that it *was* yours," Durwood answered. "Not that I'm doubting your word in the least."

"You'd be willing to let that matter be settled by a court?" Bennion asked.

"Courts are expensive and slow. I shouldn't think any of us would care to see a settlement dragged out over the years. It's been half a century already. Why throw things into litigation for another two years, say?"

"You're suggesting some kind of split?" Gail asked.

"Yes." Durwood nodded. "Some kind of equitable division of the spoils." He shrugged. "Oh, we all won't be completely satisfied. I, for example, would like everything, and no doubt each one of us would, but by taking a reasonable approach to the problem, I know we can arrive at a solution."

"What is this reasonable approach?" Bennion asked.

"That we can discuss when there seems to be a chance of recovering the loot." Durwood drew with his finger on the table. "The mile and five eighths of Hellsgrin that we're concerned with, from the bergschrund to the line between the pins that my grandfather set, moves at the rate of one hundred and seventy-one feet each year, or fifteen feet a month, or five tenths of a foot a day.

"That's over-all movement. There may be none in a given spot, more in another. We know the glacier moves. One mile and five eighths of a tremendous ice flow creeping six inches a day." Durwood shook his head and smiled. "And we are getting all excited about the next hour or two, or even the next week or two. If we should set a division figure now, all it would serve to do is to give us a long time to roll it around, and we'd each find a dozen good reasons to think we were being cheated. By the time we came to the point of actually digging something from the ice, we'd be at each other's throats. You see what I mean?"

No one said anything.

"The reasonable approach," Durwood continued, "is for each one of us to know, and believe, that he is going to get a fair shake. Without that, we're animals." He looked around with a pained expression. "And competing for something that has less than a fifty per cent chance of being found."

"Zero chance," Pancake said. His fear was gone now and he was looking at Durwood with complete fascination.

Durwood shrugged. "There you are."

Bennion tried to estimate Gail's reaction. She was at least impressed, if not convinced; and Pancake—he appeared to be believing every word. It was a fast switch, but old Pancake had proved before that he could swap ends with disconcerting suddenness.

"You've given us something to think about," Bennion said, and then realized how fatuous he sounded.

"I hope so," Durwood said. "This business of turning the horses loose and wrecking the jeep, that wasn't good." He shook his head. "Suppose we do find the gold. The best thing we could do then would be to separate and get to hell away from each other, before we became like five dogs each guarding a bone that he couldn't carry away."

"I could carry sixty pounds of gold," Tyner said.

"I doubt it," Durwood said evenly. "Perhaps Miss McBride couldn't either. Then Pancake here would have all the advantage, since he has a burro. The jackass might well become a focal point." He frowned with worried frankness. "You see, Bennion? You didn't go far enough when you wrecked the jeep and ran the horses off. You should have shot the burro. I think it's the thing to do now."

"The hell it is!" Pancake roared. "Nobody better touch Sam Harding."

"I wouldn't insist on it," Durwood said. "I'm merely trying to make a point. Is there any chance that the horses can be caught?"

Bennion shook his head. "They're halfway home now."

"Good! Maybe that will cause someone to come here, and that would relieve a situation that, believe me, I had no part in creating and didn't want under any circumstances." Durwood sighed. "That's just about the end of my contribution for the evening."

He rose. "I suggest we all think about it, what I've tried to say, I mean." He smiled at Gail. "Thanks for the coffee, Miss McBride." He started out, then turned. "There's one pre-caution that will help. Do you have a gun, Miss McBride?"

"No," Gail said.

"If you do, give it to me. I've already taken the liberty of impounding Bennion's carbine, and since we found no other weapon in the camp, I'm assuming Pancake had none. How about you, Miss McBride?"

"I have no gun," Gail said.

Bennion had risen. *Impounding!* Who the hell did Durwood think he was? Bennion made one mistake. He forgot Tyner for a moment. Tyner had been waiting. He rammed his shoulder into Bennion with neck-snapping force, driving him back to the wall.

Bennion caught the back of a chair with one hand. The chair tilted. He came close to falling and in that moment of teetering, Tyner stepped forward to hit him. Durwood's movements seemed unhurried. One instant he was two paces away from Tyner and a split second later he was within reach of the man.

Durwood caught Tyner's wrist as the blow was starting and from then on, until Tyner was on his knees, with Durwood standing above him, holding Tyner's right arm at an awkward angle, the action was too fast to follow.

"You're breaking my arm!" Tyner howled.

"That's the idea," Durwood said calmly. He showed no anger or excitement. Still holding Tyner, he looked at Gail and Pancake and Bennion. "You see what I mean? Do we want this sort of thing from now on? I can assure you that I don't."

He released Tyner suddenly and the man rose, his face twisted with pain, his left arm across his chest as he grasped his tortured shoulder. "Damn you, Durwood, you're always taking his side."

"I'm on no one's side, as I've tried to explain. I've had your version of Bennion's trying to knock you off the Hellsgrin Trail. That undoubtedly isn't the full truth of the affair, but no matter. My concern is seeing that we all act like human beings until we get our common problem settled. After that, you and Bennion can tie yourselves together and duel with broken bottles, for all I care."

For the first time Durwood showed anger.

"Don't any of you get the message? Can't you understand that for my own protection, if for no other reason, I'm trying to reduce the chances of bloodshed all I can?"

"By cornering all the guns," Bennion said.

"Yes! I've already taken the bolt from Tyner's rifle. I'll reduce your carbine to impotence and you can have it back, if you wish. Myself, I have no gun, the same as Miss McBride and Pancake. Three of us, at least, came here without violence preset in our thinking." Durwood motioned Tyner toward the door, and then he followed Tyner outside.

The three people in the room looked at each other, each wondering how much the others had been impressed by Durwood's arguments.

"The thing about disarmament," Bennion said, "is how do you know you can trust the one who does the disarming?"

"That's the whole point," Gail said. "But perhaps . . ." She glanced toward the woodbox near the stove, unconscious of the act, and Bennion thought, That's where she hid the gun.

Bennion sat down carefully. His chest was hurting. That Tyner was a bull for sure. Once he got the bulge on you, he would be mean to handle.

"He might have been telling the truth," Pancake said, as if it were a hard thought to accept.

Gail sat down. "He was convincing. I can't

argue with anything he said, if he meant it."

"He could have." Bennion frowned. Durwood was a cold one, all right, but he had to be subject to the same fears as other men, and he was aware of all the difficulties that would rise once the gold was recovered from Hellsgrin. It was like him to take a hard, practical approach to the problem.

"He might have been telling the truth," Pancake murmured.

"Do you suppose he had an even split in mind?" Gail asked. "He was shifty on that point."

"Would you split evenly?" Bennion asked.

Gail took a deep breath. "If it meant saving a killing, what else could I say but yes?" She was troubled, puzzled. "I lied to him about having a gun. He took my word. Maybe he was honest. There he was, talking about the very thing we do want to avoid, and I looked him in the eye and lied."

"I wouldn't worry about it," Bennion said. "We know our own intentions." For a moment he was about to confess his own deceit concerning one very important point, and then he decided that it was a fact which would be better held in reserve.

As if there were no others in the room, Pancake was still musing. "You can misjudge any man. He ain't got no feelings, but maybe he was on the level."

Gail said, "What do you honestly think, Johnny?"

"I don't know." There were facts that Bennion was withholding, and Pancake had some idea in his head that he would not reveal, and Bennion had suspicioned that Gail had not given all the background that she could have; and now the three of them, dishonest in their own ways, were trying to pass judgment on the honesty of Durwood.

"What do *you* think?" Bennion asked.

"I'm like you," Gail said. "You can't say he was a spellbinder, because everything he said made hard sense."

Bennion shrugged. "The obvious answer is to go along with him for a while."

"It's obvious and also crooked. We either trust him or we don't."

"Trust him?" Pancake said suddenly, as if he had just returned to the room. "I wouldn't trust the sonofabitch from here to the bar!"

ELEVEN

They worked to shave smooth windows in the ice above Point 7, all of them but Pancake, who still held stubbornly to his belief that nothing was lost in Hellsgrin. Pancake was still digging his trench.

Bennion had sharpened the ice planes with a file from the storeroom, and he had also brought a mortar hoe, which did a finer job of smoothing the ice after the initial cuts were made. At first, Durwood had tried a pick to start the cuts, but he soon learned that the impact sent fracture lines down into the ice and ruined the chances of seeing below.

For a time Tyner had worked like a fiend with his ice plane. Now he was slowing down, occasionally stopping to look around, as if he was realizing the magnitude of the task. Gail was using the second ice plane, while Durwood was finishing the windows with the finely sharpened hoe. The last action of the operation was Bennion's.

He knelt above the cuts, shading the sides of his face with his hands, changing his angle of view, trying to see into the glacier. It was an old story, full of frustration.

In a few places he could see several feet down into the misty blueness, but at most points the ice had been fractured and then rejoined until it was a mass of unseen lines and tilted planes that refracted light at so many angles that vision was impossible beyond a foot or two.

Durwood worked steadily, polishing the surface of each window with the hoe, laying a rock at each cut when he had done the job. He grew warm and took his jacket off, and that gave Bennion the chance to feel the garment as he knelt beside one of the windows. There was nothing in the pockets but a pipe and a tin of tobacco.

Tyner quit working and went over to stand by Gail. "We could be all summer doing this," he said.

Gail kept shaving away with the plane. "You're right."

"And then find nothing." Tyner gave the glacier a sullen look. "There must be some easier way than this."

"You name it and we'll try it," Gail said.

"One thing I'd like to know—how deep is the ice?"

"I've forgotten what Jackson's estimate was. Around eighty feet right here, I think."

"Jackson! I've heard enough of him to last me a lifetime." Tyner went back to work, without enthusiasm, dabbling with the ice plane, stopping to look at what the others were doing. "What are you seeing down there?" he yelled at Bennion.

"Ice," Bennion said, and he saw the quick ripple of a smile on Durwood's face.

"Always the wise guy," Tyner grumbled.

"Want to switch jobs for a while?" Bennion asked Durwood.

They changed tasks. Durwood said, "You know, if we were to sprinkle black dirt around the edges of these holes, it might help."

"It would. We can bring a sackful up tomorrow." In spite of unsettled suspicions, Bennion was beginning to respect Durwood, and he might even come to a liking for the man. "Is there such a thing as an ice scope, some kind of deal to help you see into ice?"

Durwood laughed. "I've never heard of one. It could be designed readily enough, however. I know an engineer, a Rice man, who works for the same company I do who could rig up something like that in three days. If I had been thinking, that's just what I would have had him do."

"Where's that?" Bennion asked.

"Albuquerque. AEC stuff. I was teaching college math back east before I went to work there four years ago." Durwood went over to the first window and knelt down. "Ice is right. No end of it."

After a time Tyner quit work again and began to peer into the cuts, starting at the first one they had made that morning. His fleshy face grew dark with blood each time he knelt. It was not long before he found that chore discouraging. He rose, rubbing his wet knees, scowling at the icefall farther up the glacier where Hellsgrin narrowed.

He went back to Gail to pour out his woes. "If anyone should ask, I think we're all a little crazy. I think old Pancake has a better idea than this, whatever it is."

"You can help him dig," Gail said.

"I didn't say that, but . . ." Tyner shook his head. "There're so miserable many factors involved here. How deep in the ice is that mule? We could have a window right on top of it, and if it was ten feet down, we'd never see it."

"Quite true," Gail said cheerfully.

"What are you trying to do, discourage me, doll baby?"

"You write the ticket."

"Don't worry, I'll stick around." Tyner went to the east side of the ice to gather rocks to mark the cuts. He dawdled there a long time, and when he returned he had another complaint. "How do we know someone hasn't fiddled with those steel pins during the last fifty years?"

"Measure them out," Gail said. "Jackson's survey is supposed to be accurate, and you know where zero, point, zero is."

"Jackson! Sometimes I wish it was him that had dropped in the glacier. You hear what I said, Durwood?"

Durwood grinned. "I heard you. Do like the

girl says, if you don't trust my grandfather's survey."

Tyner picked up the ice plane again.

By the middle of the afternoon the ice above Point 7 was dotted with rocks. Bennion knew that by the next day the surfaces of the windows they had cut would be minutely changed by temperature and sun, and if they wished to look into them again, the cuts would have to be thinly shaved anew.

Tyner dropped his ice plane. "I've got enough of this for one day."

The sunlight that had touched the glacier for two hours during midday was gone from the ice gorge now. It was shining strongly on the high granite ridges to the east, but here at Point 7 a coolness was descending and there was a hint of gloom, more sensed than actual.

By mutual, unspoken consent they began to leave the ice. Tyner took Gail's arm. "Come on," he said, "let's you and I go down together and let the homespun glacier scientists work out their calculations by themselves."

Durwood touched Bennion's arm in a light restraining gesture. "Nothing is going to happen to her. She could handle ten oafs like him." He studied Bennion's face keenly. "Is it a little more than just meeting a very attractive woman under unusual circumstances? Is it the *wow!* stuff?"

"Do I look like a teen-ager?"

"You certainly do not," Durwood said pleasantly. "I'm merely trying to pinpoint a possible trouble area."

"I don't want him pawing at her."

"That answers my question. Therefore, I don't want him pawing at her either."

Durwood's quiet assurance made Bennion bristle. "Who do you think you are—God?"

"No." Durwood sighed patiently. "Just a man trying to preserve his hide and get along in a ticklish situation with a minimum of trouble."

They crossed the ice and followed Tyner and Gail through the rocks.

"Who are you preserving your hide against?" Bennion asked.

"You, Tyner, Miss McBride, perhaps even Pancake, or any combination thereof. I'm a nervous man, Bennion, in spite of my poker face. This may be a great adventure to you, but I'll be glad to get away from it."

He meant it, Bennion decided. He really meant it. Maybe it was nerves that made him so cool, and fear that put the watchful stillness behind his expressions. Gail, too, had carried herself with almost perfect calmness when she was uncertain and scared.

Bennion kept pushing the descent faster, so he could keep Tyner and Gail in sight. Durwood's knee was troubling him as they scrambled over rocks. He said, "Give me a minute more, Bennion, and then go and catch up with them if you wish, although I don't think Tyner is going to gobble her up."

Bennion slowed down.

"If you haven't told Miss McBride already, I'd suggest that you keep quiet a little longer about the fact that someone has moved the drills my grandfather placed in the rocks," Durwood said. "You do know that?"

Bennion nodded.

"Was it you?"

"Yes," Bennion said. "I reset the drills a hundred and thirty-seven feet farther down the glacier the first time I came here. How did you know?"

Durwood laughed. "Not by measurement, certainly. As a matter of fact, if I hadn't compared the sides of this hole with pictures my grandfather took, I wouldn't have discovered yesterday that the icefall behind us has receded seventy or eighty feet during the last fifty years. Did you know that?"

"Yes," Bennion said. "I worked it out the hard way. The figure is closer to a hundred feet. How did you know the drills had been moved?"

Durwood stopped and put one foot up on a rock and began to massage his knee vigorously. "Grandpa Jackson was quite a character. It always irked him that he couldn't drill a nice, round hole with steel and a single-jack, like an experienced miner, which of course he wasn't. Still, it irked him when his holes always came out three-cornered. It's a matter of uniform turning of the drill between hammer blows.

"At any rate, when he put in the steel here at the glacier, he drilled his usual three-cornered holes, and he mentioned that fact in a family letter which I have, along with a great many more of his private letters." Durwood shook his head. "The holes where the drills are now are nicely rounded. I'll grant you they look as old as sin, and so do the drills, but they aren't the holes that Grandpa Jackson turned in."

"That makes me a good miner, I guess," Bennion said. "Did you tell Tyner?"

"No. Why create dissension? That's why I suggested that you don't tell Miss McBride. We're at the point of achieving a little unity of purpose which I would like to see maintained until we all scatter out of here like quail. Since you have a personal interest in Miss McBride, I think you'll agree that you might lose ground by telling her now that you've withheld information."

Durwood was right, and, therefore, irritating. They resumed the steep descent. Moving the steel markers had once seemed like a good idea, and it was, as far as thwarting the average curiosity seeker; but shortly after moving the steel, Bennion had realized that any determined man would not sit on his haunches and wait for Alonzo Pike and the golden burro to come floating right up to the surface on the exact line on the exact day.

Anyone dead serious would do just what Bennion and the others were going to do, work the ice from the *séracs* to the fall in the narrow part of the gorge, knowing that Jackson's estimate of glacier movement was undoubtedly a bit three-cornered also, like his drill holes.

Durwood was aware of those facts, so you could not say that he had any ulterior motives in suggesting that Bennion and he keep still about the pins having been moved. "You had to tell me," Bennion said. "You had to let me know that you knew about those pins."

"Yes! There was a bare chance that you didn't know, although I'll admit that I thought you were the one who changed the position of the steel." Durwood smiled. "Stop trying to analyze me. Take me at my word, consider me a slippery crook waiting to murder everybody and run away with the loot, or look at me as a man just as nervous and scared as the rest of you. But don't try to analyze me."

When they came to where they could look down on Basin City, off to the side of the last plunging fall of Hellsgrin, they saw Gail and Tyner tossing rocks out on the glacier to watch them bounce over the ice and then spin away down the mountain.

Gail laughed about something and Bennion looked down with a sour expression and Durwood said, "What do you want her to do, throw Tyner headfirst down the glacier?"

As soon as he heard voices in the town Pancake began to yell, "Ho, Johnny! John-ny, come here!"

"Maybe he's found something," Tyner said.

Pancake kept calling, his voice echoing faintly from the channels above him. Tyner and Bennion went to see what it was all about.

Pancake was still digging parts of a human skeleton from the trench. The skull and some of the other major bones lay on a flat spot at the end of the trench, brownish yellow and clotted with damp earth. Bennion knocked some of the soil from the skull. Patches of hair still clung to it, brittle, faded to dirty gray.

It would take a laboratory test, Bennion thought, to determine what color the hair had been.

"Christ!" Tyner said, peering down gingerly. "Indian?"

"Indian, your foot!" Pancake said. He began to dig vigorously, his shovel clashing on bones.

"Easy," Bennion said. "Don't bust it up."

"Nothing can hurt him now," Pancake said.

Bennion jumped down into the trench and took the shovel. "Rest a spell, Pancake."

The old man and Tyner stood on the bank while Bennion worked carefully to loosen the remaining bones from the earth. "See if you can fit them together, Tyner," Bennion said. "Then we—"

"Hell with that! What for?"

"I thought he could just be here," Pancake said. "This was one of the places the Pinkerton men didn't look. You see, this was dug in the fall. Somebody threw him into it during the winter, and by the time all the wash come off the mountain, he was plumb covered while there was still melting snow on this side of the basin."

"Who?" Tyner demanded. "Who is it?"

"I've been thinking about this trench for some time," Pancake said. "I thought—"

"Stop blabbing!" Tyner yelled. "Who is it?"

"Shut up!" Bennion said. "We don't know who it is." He thought he did though. He found fragments of rotted cloth, bits of clothing seeped down into the soil, stains rather than solid material that would hold together when handled.

Some of the bones were shattered, possibly by rocks that had rolled off the mountain. Bennion dug carefully until he had most of the major bones placed at one end of the trench. He climbed out. "How was he lying, Pancake?"

"Face down, sprawled out."

Dumped into the trench on a bitter night when snow was blowing wildly. Bennion tried not to think about it as he began to sort and place the bones. Tyner came over, watching, offering advice, now and then nudging a bone with his foot.

"What's the idea, Bennion?" he asked.

"I'm trying to get some idea of his size."

Gail and Durwood arrived just after Bennion had completed, as well as he could, the assembling of the bones.

"We were wondering what—Good Lord!" Gail said.

Durwood's expressive features showed genuine astonishment. He stared at the skeleton, at the trench, and then at Pancake. "So you were really serious, after all."

"Knowed it all the time," Pancake said. "That's most likely Alonzo Pike."

"You mean Bennion's—Well, Jesus Christ!" Tyner said. "Why didn't you say so at first?" He grinned. "There isn't much resemblance, is there?"

"You knew it all the time, Pancake?" Durwood said. "How?"

"Well, I guessed at it, I guess you could say. This is one of the places nobody looked in, as I remember, and I always said Pike never even started up Hellsgrin Trail."

Durwood nodded. "How do we prove this *is*

Pike? I can't even swear whether it's a man or woman."

"I can," Gail said. "Look at the pelvis, for one thing."

"Pike!" Tyner said. "Pike! Why then there has to be a burro here too!"

Pancake shook his head. "I wouldn't bet on that."

"Why not? The burro disappeared at the same time he did."

"Yes. Why not, Pancake?" Gail asked.

"Yeah, sure," Pancake said, "but there was burro tracks on Hellsgrin Trail. It don't make sense to think somebody led a burro clear up there and then brought him back here to kill him and hide him. Heck no! They would've dumped him into the glacier."

"I'll agree with that," Durwood said.

"Just what I always said," Pancake declared. "Somebody killed Pike, made a pass like he was going over the hill, hid the gold bars, and then laid low. There's nothing left to find."

Bennion paced two steps beside the skeleton. By that rough measurement, the man had been six feet tall. Bennion thought of taking an accurate measurement from his own height, but there was no use. All the cartilaginous structure of the skeleton was gone, so that the spine was only disassociated vertebrae, and some of the vertebrae were still in the trench.

He could be six inches off in his placement of the bones. He had neither the desire nor skill to keep on trying for a more accurate reassembly of the skeleton.

He turned to Pancake. "What other reasons make you say this is Alonzo Pike?"

"Just what I've said."

"Do you know what he was wearing when he disappeared?"

"No. I don't think nobody paid much attention to that."

"Did he wear a ring, a belt buckle—anything of metal that you remember?"

Pancake thought. He shook his head. "I don't know."

"A watch?" Gail asked.

"Ah!" Pancake wagged his finger. "A big silver watch with his name engraved inside the back."

"So if we prove this is Pike," Tyner said, "what does that tell us?"

Durwood said, "That your gold is long gone. It means that every time we fall on our tail ends up there on the glacier, we're suffering in the interests of amateur science only."

"Let's look for the watch," Gail said. She glanced at Bennion.

"I'll look," Bennion said. "After a while. You understand, Tyner, I'll do the digging where the skeleton was."

"Who gives a damn?" Tyner said. "I'm going

to start at the other end of the hole and see what's there. All the talk boils down to nobody knowing what happened around here fifty years ago. I'm going to find out."

Bennion had enough for a while. He walked toward the creek and Gail caught up with him. "What do you think, Johnny?"

"I don't know."

"If the watch is there—"

"I've got the watch at home. It was in a shop for repairs the day my grandfather disappeared."

TWELVE

Behind a long-stemmed pipe, with his blue eyes crinkled in a thoughtful expression, Durwood did indeed look like the college math teacher he said he once had been. Excepting Tyner, who said he was not hungry and had chosen to stay and dig in the trench, they were all at the table in the Nose Paint.

It was Gail's idea that they have coffee and sandwiches together, although no one professed to be hungry, until after he sat down and saw food. Now they were waiting for a second pot of coffee.

"Pancake, where's the other places the Pinkerton men overlooked?" Durwood asked.

"A watershaft over near the Yankee mill and an old caved-in tunnel near the Midas. They put grapple hooks down the shaft, but they didn't unwater it for a real good look."

"I see." Durwood turned his head to blow smoke away from the table. "How about the tunnel—was it caved in 1909?"

"Some," Pancake said. "It's plumb caved now. I ain't sure whether them Pinkertons looked in it or not, but I always sort of doubted it."

Bennion was only half listening as he struggled with a few private speculations occasioned by the discovery of the skeleton. If it was his grandfather, then Alonzo Pike had not been a thief, a family deserter, a fugitive, but an innocent man and a victim of murder.

That of course was what Bennion wanted to believe, but all his theories wrecked against one hard rock of fact: Pike himself had got the burro; no one had forced him to do that. And he had given the stableman no explanation of why he needed a burro on a stormy evening when the citizens of Basin City were huddled around their stoves.

Durwood's voice cut into Bennion's speculation. "If it really is Pike, there goes a beautiful bit of glacier history."

That was the hard point: How could it ever be proved who the skeleton was? Bennion rose suddenly and went to the storeroom to find a wooden box.

"No doubt, Miss McBride," Durwood was saying, "you've had access at some time to the investigation reports, so perhaps you can clear up something that's been troubling me. I've been wondering who was entrusted with the combination of the mill safe, besides Pike."

"Peyton Shores, who was the general manager, Victor Shores, and Peleg Lockwood."

"Who was Lockwood?" Durwood asked.

Bennion was emptying mine rail spikes and fishplates from a box. He stopped and listened.

"He was the mill foreman," Gail said. "Afterward, he was superintendent of the mill."

"That's interesting," Durwood said. "He must have been extremely well trusted to get the job, when he must have been a suspect right after the robbery."

"He was, and so was Pike—well trusted, I mean. Lockwood was cleared almost immediately because for two days he hadn't been near the safe room. He'd been working at the upper level of the mill, where they were having trouble with freezing water lines."

"I see." Durwood paused. "All these people are dead now?"

"All of them," Gail said. "No, that's wrong. Peleg Lockwood is still living, at Bennion's ranch."

Bennion dumped the box and walked out of the storeroom. "Lockwood thinks the same as Pancake, Pike didn't rob the safe." He went back to the storeroom for a shovel.

"Where you going with that?" Pancake asked.

"To give Tyner a hand." It occurred to Bennion that he should not have left Tyner over there in the trench alone; Tyner might have shoveled away something that would identify the skeleton.

"Tell him I'll bring some coffee over in a few minutes," Gail said.

Tyner was not digging where the skeleton had been. He had started at the other end of the wash that filled the trench, and it was evident by the work he had done that he was more enthusiastic about this exploration than the difficult job of probing Hellsgrin.

He was almost civil, for a change. "Pancake doesn't want anyone digging here, and that leads me to think the gold may be close."

"That's the way to find out," Bennion said. But he knew that if Pancake had had even a strong hunch about gold being in the trench, he would have dug it up years before.

Working slowly and deliberately, Bennion spaded out the ground where the skeleton had been, spreading the dirt thinly on the rocky bottom of the trench behind him. He watched each shovelful and when he saw anything that looked unusual, he raked through the backfill with a stick.

He found the rusted brass top of a small leather purse. The next shovelful he spread across the bottom of the trench showed little reddish balls of earth, and when he broke the first one open he had a twenty dollar gold piece. He found nine more coins of the same denomination.

"Anything over there?" Tyner called.

"Nothing much."

Just before Gail arrived with a thermos of coffee, Bennion found a small pocketknife rusted into a lump, and another encrusted piece of metal that was too lumpy to identify. He showed the pocketknife to Gail and Tyner. "You're wasting time," Tyner said. He wiped sweat from his forehead and grinned at Gail when she gave him coffee. "Always thinking of me, hey, dreamboat?"

Tyner tried the coffee, but it did not stop him very long. Before he had finished a cupful, he went back to shoveling.

Bennion leaned against the bank and scraped with his knife at the small object he had not yet identified. Gail leaned down to watch him. The metal took shape under his paring. It was nothing but a small, flat piece about two inches long. Until the encrusted dirt broke away in the middle and left a round hole, Bennion had no idea what he was holding.

He looked at Gail. "Maybe if we wash it off in the creek a little—"

Tyner stuck his head up. "What is it?"

"I think it's a piece of suspender buckle," Gail said, and Tyner grunted and went back to work.

Gail and Bennion went down to the river. "It's a cigar cutter," Bennion said. "Some men used to carry them in their pockets." He cut into the metal with his knife point. "That's gold."

"Did your grandfather smoke cigars?"

"He didn't smoke anything."

"It's possible that some friend who didn't know that gave it to him. Men carry a lot of unnecessary things in their pockets."

"Yeah," Bennion said, and showed Gail the nine gold coins. "Having that much money in his pocket is just not in character with what I've heard of Alonzo Pike."

"Maybe he won it gambling and was holding out on his wife."

Bennion shook his head. "No. He didn't gamble. Peleg Lockwood told me that."

"You don't think it's your grandfather. I was hoping it was."

"Why?"

"Because it means so much to you to prove him innocent."

"I never said it did."

Gail smiled. "I know, but I'm sure it does."

"That would mean there's no gold to find."

"Yes," Gail said with positive emphasis. "That might be a blessing to us all. I'm still afraid of what's going to happen if we should find it."

"What is it?" Tyner yelled from the trench.

"A suspender clip," Bennion said. He looked Gail in the eye and told her about moving the steel pins at the glacier, and how Durwood had found out about it.

"It didn't make a great deal of difference, did it?" she said, and gave him a long, serious look. "Johnny, is there any chance that Pancake is your grandfather?"

"I've been thinking about that. Peleg Lockwood didn't recognize him. Of course, Peleg is nearly blind. I don't know, Gail. I don't think he is, but I couldn't prove it any more than I can prove who that skeleton is, and I don't think that's Alonzo Pike either."

Gail frowned. "He takes such a protective interest in you, and lately, I notice he has the same attitude toward me."

"That's no evidence."

"I can't do this all by myself!" Tyner yelled.

"How were you going to identify your grandfather if you found him in the glacier?"

"A wedding ring," Bennion said. "A wedding ring engraved inside the band."

"Pancake wore a wedding ring, until a short time ago, or a ring, at least. The mark is still on his finger."

Bennion stared at her. "I never noticed that."

"You look close."

Tyner yelled again for help. Gail glanced toward the hill with an irritated expression. "Being nice to him in the interests of Durwood's big unity program is a trying business."

"Be careful how nice you are to him."

"Don't forget my thermos bottle," Gail said, and started back toward camp. Saber, who had been consorting with Sam Harding, came plunging up the creek to meet her.

As Bennion went back toward the trench, he saw Pancake and Durwood going toward the Yankee mill.

"About time somebody came back to help me," Tyner said. "I think I've found something."

He had. It was, as near as Bennion could tell, the rib bone of a burro.

Near the upper end of the millpond of the Yankee Blade, Durwood and Pancake threw aside warped boards and sheets of crumpled tin until they uncovered a caved-in shaft collar. It was filled with water to the surface.

"That's it," Pancake said. "They used to pump water from it for the mill, when the crick was flooding and all dirty. Most of the time it was boarded over, and then the mill fell in and nobody even knew the hole was here."

"But it was accessible when the Pinkerton men were searching," Durwood said. He leaned forward cautiously to look at the old shaft.

"Sure," Pancake said, "but all they did was dabble some grapple hooks down there. That's fifty feet deep and there's a drift goes east from the bottom."

Durwood shook his head and backed away. "I don't like that view. Let's take a look at the old strong room."

Pancake hesitated for an instant and then he said, "Sure."

Durwood let the old man go first through the arched doorway. Pancake walked over and kicked the safe. "Somebody blew the back end out of it years ago. The inside is full of rat nests."

"See if the door will open."

"It's locked. That's why somebody blowed the back."

"Try it," Durwood said.

Pancake gave him a startled look, and then the old man reached down and tried the handle. "I said it was locked."

Looking past his pipe as he held a match to the bowl, Durwood put one foot up on a fallen chunk of masonry, and said quietly, "Open it, Pancake."

"Open . . ." Pancake turned white.

"Turn the dial to the right numbers and open it." Durwood dropped the match on the floor. His eyes never left Pancake's face.

"What are you talking about?"

"About opening the safe. You can do it. Don't try to remember the numbers. Just do it from habit, without thinking."

"Are you nuts?" Pancake said, but there was no steam in his voice.

Durwood was only partly blocking the arched doorway. The other end of the safe room was completely open, except for tumbled masonry. There was nothing threatening in Durwood's stance, or even in his expression. It was the cold sureness of his voice that made Pancake feel like a man trapped.

"I ain't no Jimmy Valentine," the old man said. "If you want it open, get somebody with sandpapered fingers."

"The mechanism seems to be intact. Open it, Pancake," Durwood said, quietly and persuasively.

Pancake turned as if he intended to go scrambling away over the broken masonry behind the safe, and then the toughness in him asserted itself and he said loudly, "I think you're plumb crazy!" He stamped out, passing close to Durwood, who made no move to stop him.

Once outside, Pancake stopped and shouted angrily, "That's your whole trouble, you're crazy! I ain't showing you anything more about this camp!"

Bennion heard the angry yell. He leaped up on the dirt pile to look. He saw Pancake heading for the freight yard, and Durwood lounging in the doorway of the safe room.

"Come on, come on," Tyner said impatiently. "Let's get this hole cleaned out."

A little later Durwood came over to the trench. He stared like a man bemused when he saw the new find. "That really is a jackass, isn't it?"

"I'd say so," Bennion said. "Get Pancake over here. He can tell us for sure."

"Pancake is a little upset right now. I asked him to open that old safe and he was highly insulted."

"Oh?" Bennion said. "You think he isn't L. G. Riddle?"

"I did have some ideas along that line."

Durwood looked at the bones of the burro and then at the wooden box where Bennion had placed the parts of the human skeleton. "I'm a little confused. You know, Bennion, I'm beginning to think we're about fifty years too late to get rich on anything we find in this whole basin."

"All the talk isn't helping any," Tyner said. "What we need is more help digging."

"That's odd," Durwood said. "I felt the same way up there on the glacier today." He looked at his watch. "I think it's rather late to pursue this operation further today, don't you fellows?"

"I'll go for that." Bennion jammed his shovel into the bank. It was well after sundown.

Tyner stopped and looked at the sky. He was sweating heavily and his grizzled mustache was smeared with dirt. "We could bring some gas lanterns over and—"

"I don't go for double shifts." Bennion picked up the thermos. He and Durwood walked away. Bennion stopped at the creek to scour his hands with sand and water.

Tyner had climbed out of the trench by then, but he was still reluctant to leave.

"He's hoping but he certainly isn't thinking," Durwood said. "Still, I suppose we'd better help him shovel out the trench tomorrow. By the way, did you find anything that would tend to identify the man?"

"No."

Durwood looked up toward the glacier. He shook his head. "Well, it's been an interesting vacation."

"You mean you're quitting?"

"No, I'll stick around, but finding the man and the burro just about clinches it, wouldn't you say?"

Bennion said, "If it's Alonzo Pike, yes."

"Of course it's impossible to prove that, right here on the spot."

"How could you prove it anywhere?"

"An expert in legal medicine could determine the man's age, height, and other physical characteristics. You'd be surprised what those boys can do."

They went on toward town. Tyner was still standing at the trench.

"Don't you think the burro is enough proof?" Durwood asked.

"I don't know." It seemed to Bennion that he had been giving that answer from the first day he came to Basin City.

"It's just about enough for me," Durwood said.

They were a few buildings away from Durwood's quarters before he spoke again. "Let's get your carbine, Bennion. I must have appeared stupid and unbearable when I set myself up as administrator of affairs for Basin City and environs."

He led Bennion into a sagging building and retrieved the carbine from behind a heavy sled leaning against the wall. "I didn't do anything to it."

Bennion checked that statement. The barrel was clear, the mechanism was untouched, and there were still cartridges in the magazine.

"Now Tyner's rifle is a different matter," Durwood said. "I've hidden the bolt and I'm not going to return it as long as he has any whiskey left. He's got plenty." He smiled. "Accept my apologies for playing God?"

"Forget it," Bennion said. "By the way, I told Gail about moving the drills."

"Oh? And how did she take it?"

"The same as you."

"Good! Now we're getting somewhere. We're being honest with each other." Then Durwood added, "Of course I see no need to strain ourselves and tell Tyner about your little deception, since it's proved of no consequence and would only increase his dislike for you."

"The feeling is mutual," Bennion said.

THIRTEEN

The trench lay exposed down to solid rock and out to the walls of the original excavation. Using a piece of grating from the Golden Hoof mill, Bennion had screened the earth where the human skeleton had lain. His findings were in the wooden box, five corroded brass buttons, part of a boot heel and a small, flat bottle.

Tyner had turned up the rest of the burro, a crosstree saddle rotted down to slender oaken sticks, fragments of brittle leather, and an assortment of harness rings and buckles. He stood on the dirt pile, angry and puzzled.

"You really didn't expect to find the bars there, did you?" Durwood asked.

Tyner gave him a bitter look. "At least I tried to find something, while the rest of you dabbled around and talked." He started away, taking Gail by the arm. "Let's you and me have a drink and talk this over."

"No thanks."

"Come on! Come on! There's nothing—"

"I said no thank you." Gail pulled her arm free.

Tyner strode away, and Bennion thought, He'll get gassed to the ears. I hope he's disgusted enough to leave.

Pancake sat on the dirt and shook his head at

189

the burro bones. "That's the last thing I expected to find."

Durwood picked one of the buttons from the box. He scraped at it with a knife. "From a pair of overalls, isn't it?"

"Looks like it," Bennion said.

"That's Pike," Pancake said. "That sure as shooting is." He stood up. "I'm going fishing."

"We all should," Durwood said dryly. "Pancake, was there anyone else besides Pike who disappeared in Basin City?"

"None I knew of that wasn't accounted for in some way. Basin City wasn't like Leadville, where every spring you were like to find twenty men that had been murdered and throwed out in the snow. This was a decent place to live, except for the winters. We had a fire system here, plugs and all, and a fire company—" Pancake stopped suddenly. "Hell with that fire company."

He walked away, and before he reached the creek he was singing "In the Shadow of the Pines." Saber fell in with him. Sunning himself by the corner of the pasture, Sam Harding turned his head lazily to watch them go.

Bennion saw Durwood staring at the burro. Some quick leaping thought struck Durwood hard, and it was as though he had said, "Ah!" And then Durwood looked down toward the beaver ponds and said, "I think Pancake has the right idea. Do you happen to have a fishing rod I could borrow, Miss McBride?"

"A spinning rod."

"That'll do fine."

Bennion stayed after they left. He looked at the box of human bones and considered burying them where they had been found, but he did not do it; he gathered boards and covered the box and weighted it with rocks, and then he waited until Pancake began to fish in the Golden Hoof millpond. . . .

Old Pancake complained, "You're worse than the dog when it comes to scaring the fish."

There was, as Gail had said, the mark of a ring on one of Pancake's fingers.

"Dealer Dan Powell disappeared from here," Bennion said. "Do you remember that?"

"Dealer Dan?" Pancake missed a strike. "Damn it! You interrupt a man's fishing, Johnny." He whaled the line out again with his old steel rod. "Dan, yeah, he disappeared. He owed Queenie about three thousand bucks, and everybody else in town besides. He sure did disappear. Somebody seen him afterward in Arizona, and then I heard later he got rich on real estate in Los Angeles."

"You don't think he got dumped in that hole we just dug out?"

"What?" Pancake let his line go slack.

"That's what I said."

"Hell! Dealer Dan would've looked good in overalls, and that's what those buttons you found came from." Pancake reached out and touched Bennion's forehead. "You got a fever, boy?"

"What happened to the ring you used to wear, Pancake?"

Pancake held his left hand out. "It got so loose I took it off to keep from losing it again. It came off once when I was digging a hole up near Cameron Park and it took me a half day to find it. What are you trying to do, give me the third degree, Johnny?" The old man's eyes were puzzled, troubled.

"I'm just trying to figure things out."

"You got Lonnie Pike over there in a box. You've got the burro. That's about all there is to it, as I see it. Go think up some more questions if you want, but leave me alone until I catch a mess of fish, will you?"

"One more question. What did you do with the ring?"

Pancake sighed. "It's over in my pack, in that little sack where I carry salve and stuff. Go look at it."

Bennion did look at the ring. It was worn thin, a wide wedding band of gold. Faintly, beyond reading, marks of engraving still showed.

Time. That was the barrier that frustrated every idea Bennion had.

He saw Durwood going down the road toward the beaver ponds.

Gail was opening tin cans. The room was hot from the fire in the big cookstove. "I don't think I'd ever get used to cooking on that thing," Gail said. "It uses a hundred thousand B.T.U.'s to heat a can of soup."

"Every woman should be required to go through a probationary period of six months with one of those ranges, before being turned loose on a husband who has to supply her with all the modern conveniences."

"The hell you say! How many wives have you had?"

"Five or six," Bennion said. He retreated from the heat of the stove and sat down at the poker table. "Bring on the chow!"

"All right, lout. I was going to ask you anyway, since all the decent citizens have gone fishing. What did you find out from Pancake?"

"Nothing. I saw his wedding ring. It reminded me of what Durwood said, we're fifty years too late." Bennion told her of his conversation with Pancake. "I just don't see him as my grand-father."

"You could ask him directly."

"Yeah, and he'd slide away into a story about Aztec buried treasure or the Lost Dutchman mine or how to run a crooked faro game. The only way we'll ever find out who Pancake really is will be when he decides to tell the truth, if he ever does."

They began to eat. "Good soup," Bennion said. "When we eat up all your chow, I may let you have some of mine."

"Thanks. I've already had that offer from Tyner, more graciously too, I might add."

"I'll match any promise he makes, and then double it."

"I feel sorry for Tyner," Gail said. "I think he's about ready to quit."

"Bully!"

"What about Durwood—will he quit?"

Bennion thought about it. "No. He's puzzled, and for a while he was really thrown off, but now I think he's come around to the same thought as me."

"And what's that?"

"That burro Tyner found is a fake. Somebody planted it there."

Gail did not press the subject until she had finished eating. "All right, how do you know it was planted?"

"Clean bones," Bennion said. "Absolutely clean bones. If that burro had been dumped in the hole with a heavy winter coat of hair, there still would have been patches of hair all through the dirt, wads of it. At first, it didn't strike me, not until I screened some of the dirt."

Gail glanced toward the doorway. "Durwood mentioned that too?"

"No. I saw him looking at Sam Harding, and all of a sudden his face lit up like a pinball machine."

"That's a tricky business, reading minds, Johnny."

"I wasn't reading his mind, I was reading his expression."

"And he didn't say anything?"

"No . . . By the way, he's given me back my carbine." Bennion went to the stove for coffee.

"If he doesn't say anything about it, then I'll really be worried," Gail said, "because, so far, Durwood has been completely honest."

"Honest, or disarming."

"Honest," Gail said. "He can't hide anything behind that face, although he bragged to me about having a poker face."

"Maybe he has, but not the blank kind." Bennion lit a match while Gail was still getting a cigarette out of the pack. She watched him with curious intentness as he held it to her cigarette.

"Who put the burro there?" she asked. "Pancake?"

"He seemed as surprised as anyone to see it."

"I know. He can cover up until you don't know what he's thinking. I'll swear he isn't L. G. Riddle. Let me show you something else about L. G. Riddle." Gail went behind the bar and got the file of the *Basin Advocate*. She had marked her place with a whiskey label, *Blackie Tedrow's Nose Paint, Special Proof for High Altitudes.*

Bennion picked up the label. "It's still gummed. I never saw one of those before."

"I found a whole roll of them jammed in a crack," Gail said. She put the file on the table. "Read that."

It was a filler from the issue of June 14, 1909.

Mr. L. G. Riddle, the estimable proprietor and sole resident of Boiler Manor, sometimes known as Pancake, is again in a legal mood. This time he is threatening to sue several parties because of the recent incident in Queenie's Place. To the hilt, as usual.

Gail turned to another marker and indicated the story.

Your editor is now in danger of legal annihilation. Two weeks ago we called Mr. L. G. Riddle estimable. When he inquired the meaning thereof, we told him it meant esteemed, and he said, by Ned, there was no steam left at Boiler Manor. Again, he may sue. To the you-know-what.

"Real funny, that editor," Bennion said, but he knew that the remarks were in the broad, rough mood of the time when they were written.

"There are other stories like that," Gail said. "They seem to prove that Riddle, whoever he may have been, was here in town during the summer of 1909, not prospecting as Pancake says he was."

"He could have been in and out," Bennion said absently, but he did not hold it to be much of a point. The real evidence about Pancake Riddle was the character implied by the editor.

Gail said, "Obviously, Riddle was the town clown, a real offbeat joker. He wasn't the Pancake we know. Our Pancake throws out a terrific verbal smokescreen, but his head is sound."

Bennion had been avoiding any decision about Pancake for some time. If Pancake was not who he said he was, and that was almost a fact, then his reasons for being here created a new field of distrust. He then became no longer an ally, and perhaps a deadly enemy.

Bennion said, "He's not Riddle, and the skeleton he 'found' is not Alonzo Pike."

"Then we're still with the glacier version?"

"We have no other choice. Have you got any other idea?"

Gail shook her head. "Maybe Pancake was one of the principals in the robbery."

"I've kicked that around too. If he was, why should he be afraid to tell his real name now? Why would he wait fifty years, like the rest of us? He's been coming over here five or six years already, and if there was anything to find, he would have had it before this, wouldn't he?" Bennion spread his hands in a gesture of helplessness.

"There's one sure place, at least that we know about, where we couldn't have recovered the gold before this—if it's even possible now," Gail said.

"Sure, the glacier. So that puts Pancake back in a class with the rest of us, with no reason to lie about his real identity."

Gail kept looking at him and Bennion knew what she was thinking, so he said it. "Unless he's my grandfather, which I don't buy. I know, the burro fell into the bergschrund and Pike got away. So he waits, like everyone else, for Hellsgrin to move a mile and five eighths, and in the meantime he tries to discourage the rest of us by digging up a skeleton of a man and the burro bones, hoping we'll all go home and leave him easy pickings on the glacier. Does that make sense?" As soon as he said it, Bennion wished he had not; it did make sense.

Gail's look said the same thing.

Bennion was on the defensive when he asked, "Who else close to that robbery could still be living? Peleg Lockwood, yes. He isn't here. How about Victor Shores?"

"Oh nuts! I've got pictures of his funeral procession. One of my aunts never did quit

198

talking about what a fine send-off they gave him."

"All right, take P. R. Shores."

"He was drowned at Lido long before I was born. He was . . ." Gail hesitated.

"He was what?"

"Well, that's family history we don't talk about."

"Let's have it, along with the pictures of his funeral procession."

"He was the black sheep of the family," Gail said. "He went through a pile of money with various wildcat deals and then he married into money and kept right on wheeling. The Yankee Blade was the only thing he was ever involved in that paid off, but, even then, Victor Shores had to spend his summers here to keep an eye on the family's interests."

"You mean P. R. was dipping into the till?" Bennion said.

"I don't know that. Maybe it was inefficiency and extravagance that Victor was trying to prevent. I know Victor had a fit when P. R. donated a waterworks to Basin City, out of Yankee profits." Gail hesitated. "Yes, I have heard my aunt hint darkly that P. R. was a bit sticky fingered."

"What happened to him after he left here?"

"He and his wife went back to Pennsylvania and he went to work for his father-in-law in the banking business. He sort of fouled up there too. His personal life was shady, it seems. He liked too many women, of all kinds. According to my family, his finest hour was when he drowned in Europe."

"There's no doubt about it?"

Gail shrugged. "He's buried at Lido. I've seen his grave."

Bennion stood up. "You don't have to tell me. Alonzo Pike is the only one unaccounted for." He started out.

"Where are you heading now?"

"I'm going to jump in the bergschrund."

The door of Tyner's cabin was open. Tyner was on his bunk, with a bottle of whiskey on a chair beside him. He was either sound asleep or passed out. Bennion went on to where he was clear of the buildings and could see down the creek.

Durwood and Pancake had covered a lot of ground. They were far away, fishing from the dam of the same beaver pond. Pancake's shiny steel rod glinted in the sun as he cast. Regular fishing chums, after all that talk of Pancake's about not trusting Durwood. . . .

Bennion turned around. He could talk to Pancake later, not that it would do much good. Tyner was still sacked out like a waterlogged timber. Maybe there was some merit in that, Bennion thought; at least it kept your brain from trying to wring answers out of problems that seemed to have no answers.

He got a bucket from the storeroom. "You want to go up on Hellsgrin?" he asked Gail.

"Not this afternoon. Since I've got the stove fired up, I'm going to take advantage of it and wash some clothes."

Bennion filled the bucket with fine, black earth from a corner of the freight yard. It might work, that idea of Durwood's about using dirt to kill the light reflection around the edges of the windows in the glacier. He thought of something else that likely had no value at all, but was worth a try: He got his binoculars.

In the slow grind of time Hellsgrin would spill everything it carried. Every rock that fell into the bergschrund would emerge someday on the outfall, and if Stony Jackson had been right in his calculations of the glacier's movement, in approximately four years Alonzo Pike, Whingding and the burro's golden burden would appear at the terminal end of Hellsgrin.

Before starting the hard climb into the rocks to get around the final plunge of the glacier, Bennion rested, looking at the tremendous icefall. Four years. From his point in time, four years loomed larger than the fifty already past.

The rocks that stood in melting hollows on the icefall looked like the same rocks he had seen last year, and like the rocks he had seen the first time he ever came here. He knew how great the odds were against finding Alonzo Pike before Hellsgrin itself gave the body up.

That was the way it had been with the eleven men led by the British doctor who had all been swept by an avalanche into a glacier on Mount Blanc in 1820. Forty-one years later and nearly four miles away, they had been released by the ice.

But there was also Lord Francis Douglas, another Briton, who in 1865 fell three thousand feet down the Matterhorn into a crevasse. Scientists said his body would emerge in eighty-four years, but that calculation did not come true.

Bennion went on up into the rocks with his bucket of black soil. He stopped at the last break where he could look down on the basin. Pancake and Durwood were barely visible; they were on the old road, going farther away beside the beaver ponds.

He climbed on until he could see the ice field of the glacier, and then caution that had sharpened into distrust during the last few days caused him to put the bucket down and go back to where he could look between the rocks and see the basin again. He used the binoculars.

Pancake and Durwood were even farther away, fishing once more. He saw Tyner standing in front of the cabin, looking up at the glacier, Tyner who had been asleep when Bennion left, or too drunk to move.

Tyner moved now. He went behind the cabin to look at something toward the creek. Bennion swung the glasses. Saber was down by the creek with Sam Harding. Tyner turned and went up the street to the Nose Paint.

He staggered when he crossed the porch. He went inside and shut the door.

Bennion started back to Basin City as fast as he could.

FOURTEEN

Gail was washing clothes in a tub set on two chairs near the stove. Her first reaction was disgust when Tyner lurched into the room with a bottle of whiskey in his hand. A moment later it was fear, when Tyner closed the door and looked for a catch or bar to hold it fast.

There was none. He shouldered the door hard against its stops and tried the knob without turning it. That satisfied him.

"Well, doll baby," he said, "I came to give you that little drink you promised to take."

The fumes were in his brain. His eyes were mean and there was an ugly grin on his lips. Gail judged him quickly. He was still responsible. She could handle him if she was careful. "How about a cup of coffee first?"

"Save it for Bennion. I said we'd have whiskey. You're going to drink a whole bottle, remember?"

Gail's lips felt stiff but she managed a smile. "That promise was made under duress, remember?"

"Under duress," Tyner said thickly. "What does she look like under duress?" He laughed. "You washing any dur-esses in that tub?" That was even funnier to Tyner.

"I'll get some glasses." Gail shook water from

her hands and turned to get a towel on the wall near the stove. She was close to the woodbox. The gun was hidden there, wrapped in a piece of canvas.

No. That would be foolish. She would have the drink, talk to him, get him out of the room after a bit.

"What does she look like under duress?" Tyner stood between the poker table and the bar, scraping at the neck of the bottle with a knife. He tried to lance the foil around the cork and cut himself. He snapped blood off his finger and cursed.

Gail moved over to the cupboard to get glasses.

"Never mind," Tyner said. "I'm getting used to drinking out of cups." He lurched over to the table and sat down, twisting at the cork until it broke loose from the foil.

There was still some coffee in the cups that Bennion and Gail had drunk from. Tyner poured one cup into the other and then threw the contents over his shoulder. He scowled. "Which one was his?"

With one hand on the cupboard shelf, Gail glanced at the woodbox. She wished she could keep from doing that; there was no need to be panicky. If she had the gun in her hand, and needed it, she was doubtful that she could use it. Not after seeing what it had done to a cactus at close range.

"Bring two more cups!" Tyner ordered. He swept the cups on the table with his hand and they rolled over to the bar. "I'm not drinking from anything that bastard had his mouth on!"

There was a moment as she went toward the table when Gail considered running toward the door. It would be close, what with the way the door stuck, but she might be able to make it and get outside and call Saber, if he hadn't wandered too far away with Pancake.

That too was panic. She had coped with Tyner before; she could do it again. She sat down across the table from him. He poured the cups almost full, measuring one against the other with drunken deliberateness.

When he looked up at her, she caught a full view of the darkness in Tyner's mind. He was drunk, yes, and he would get drunker and that would be his excuse, but he knew what he was doing and he knew what he had planned before he came into the room, and that made him responsible for his lust, responsible and terrifying.

She held tight against the fear that rose in her after that one clear look. She wiped moisture from her forehead and said, "It's hot in here. I think I'll open the door." She was moving as she spoke, naturally and without haste.

It almost worked. And then Tyner came out of his chair with the same ease and quickness that had surprised her when he grabbed her up and swung her over the bergschrund that day on Hellsgrin Trail. He caught her shoulder and swung her around and sent her reeling back toward the stove.

"What's the score, doll baby? Don't like my company?"

"I was only going to let some fresh air—"

"Along with the dog? Was that it, doll baby?"

Gail sat down again.

"That's better," Tyner said. He picked up his cup and stood with one foot on a chair, looking down at her. "You and me got nothing to beef about, have we?"

"No, I guess we haven't."

"You guess? You damn' well better know it. Try it again, doll baby. You're not going to fight with me, are you?"

The look in Tyner's eyes, his tone, was sickening, and every time he said "doll baby" it was like dragging sand across raw nerves.

"Say it!" he said.

"All right, we've got nothing to fight about."

"That's good. I can get awful rough when I have to." Tyner started to raise the cup. Some of the whiskey slopped over the edge. He lowered the cup and said, "How was Bennion, the pure and noble cowboy?"

"What do you mean?"

Tyner put the cup on the table. He leaned out swiftly and slapped Gail a rocking blow that made her see white flashes. "Let's don't be cute, doll baby. He's been spending his afternoons here talking over the guided missile program, has he? How was he?"

Gail stared at him.

"You'd better answer me."

She didn't answer. Tyner feinted another slap and she threw her head back. He laughed. "Never mind. You'll know the difference. I'm a real man and I don't kiss horses."

Foul, Gail thought; the foulest brute I ever knew passing himself as a man. And it was not all the whiskey's fault. His hand almost encircled the cup when he grasped it again.

"Drink up, doll baby. We'll have this one, and then another one, and then we'll get fundamental." Tyner stepped around the table. He grasped her by the shoulder, pressing harder and harder while she fought to keep from wincing or crying out.

He released her suddenly and stepped away, grinning. "You're not afraid. Don't try to put on an act for me. I startled you a little, yes, but deep down you're not one bit afraid. You're wondering and you're waiting—and you're ready. That's the truth, isn't it?"

Gail picked up the cup of whiskey. "Yes, I'm waiting."

Tyner laughed. "Then there's no hurry, see?" He began to pour his cup full again. "Wait a minute! You're way behind, way behind. You wouldn't want me to pour that down your pretty little throat, would you?"

"No, I wouldn't." Gail sipped the drink. The first few drops were like fire against the tightness and dryness of her throat. She coughed and her eyes watered.

"Drink it!" Tyner yelled. "Don't give me that dainty act of sipping. I'll bet you've knocked off enough double shots at one sitting to put me under the table."

She tried to be deliberate and sure when she threw the whiskey at his face. Her mind was working coolly enough then but her hand and arm hurried the movement. The liquid caught only the side of Tyner's face instead of his eyes.

Tyner grabbed the back of her shirt as she leaped past him. "Why, goddamn you!" he said, and started to drag her back. She tore the shirt as she twisted and flung herself toward the door and when the material gave way she almost fell.

There was no time to make the door. She ran behind the bar. Tyner sized that game up quickly after he made one try to catch her. She came back into the room and feinted with him, with the bar between them. When he came around the end of the long counter, she was going around the other. He made a quick reverse and they faced each other from opposite ends of the bar.

"Well," Tyner said, "that's an interesting little

game, but I'm not going to play it." He went back to the table and sat down. "Come on out and have your drink, and then I'll leave."

Gail looked at the door. It was too far. It was too hard to open. That's what he wanted her to try. She stayed where she was.

"Hell, someone is likely to come in any minute," Tyner said. "What are you afraid of?"

Durwood and Bennion were the only ones likely to come to the Nose Paint, if they were close, but they were not close. Bennion would probably stay all afternoon at the glacier, and Durwood, when he borrowed the fishing rod, said he was going clear to the head of the canyon. And Pancake, there was no telling where he was.

Tyner took a gulp of whiskey. "Scared, huh? No need to be, doll baby. I'm leaving, and I'll leave you the bottle to show that my heart's in the right place."

He went to the door and put his hand on the knob. "No hard feelings?"

By then Gail was at the far end of the bar.

"Well . . ." Tyner said, and then he came charging down the room with his face contorted with fury.

She did not know which way he would go, behind the bar or in front of it, so she had to stay where she was, poised to jump either right or left. Tyner went down the outside of the bar. Gail ran in the opposite direction, with the bar between them.

Tyner's try was almost good. He flung himself up on the bar when they were about to pass each other on opposite sides. He made a long reach and Gail almost ran right into his hands. At the last instant she ducked and went skidding on her hands and knees. The feel of Tyner's hands on top of her head and on her shoulders was still with her when she leaped up.

That would not happen again. From now on she would press close to the backbar, where he could not reach her.

Tyner slid off the bar. He called her names that dripped with filth, but they came through her desperation with no meaning and no power to offend or hurt her.

"I'll catch you," Tyner said, "and then I'm not going to be gentle, like I intended." He went back to the whiskey, but this time he did not take a drink. He swung away from the table and went to the woodbox.

The first stick of wood missed her head by a narrow margin. She thought she had been afraid before, but Tyner's new attempt added a notch of terror. He was going to stun her if he could and then take her. He picked up another stick of wood.

He tried to feint her into running one way along the bar while he went the other way, and

211

then he would have her at close range. When she outguessed him by doubling back quickly, he still almost got her with the heavy piece of wood. It broke a backbar mirror close to her shoulder.

If he kept up that attack, he would get her, she knew. She had been considering trying to crash through the front window, but the thought of cutting her face hideously had stopped her. She overcame that revulsion; if Tyner kept throwing wood, she would have to try the window.

And then she remembered the whistle in the small case on the bar. She had been running back and forth past it all this time. Saber might hear it; he had heard it before across great distance. It was desperation because he could not get in if he did come, but his raging at the door would give Tyner something to think about.

The bag was at the end of the bar close to the woodbox, and Gail was at the other end.

Tyner picked up another heavy stick of wood. She could see the dark brown streaks of pitch in it, and she knew how solid it was. She set herself to run toward the window.

Then Tyner struck upon another idea. He tossed the stick of wood away and walked to the middle of the bar, and then he dropped in front of it, out of sight. The sudden quietness of the room was a shock. A moment later Gail heard a plank creak.

She stepped out to peer around the end of the bar. Tyner was coming toward her, squatted low, with his hands on the floor. She flung herself back around the bar to run and then she hesitated. That was what he wanted her to do. He would double back.

She forced herself to stand still, listening, but she could not hear Tyner. If she let him get to the end of the bar, the same end close to her, he would lunge around it and she could not outrun him. Where was he? Had he doubled back, or was he still coming toward the front end of the room?

Gail pressed against the backbar as she went on tiptoe, moving to a position midway along the bar. That was her best protection until she knew where Tyner was. Not seeing him, not hearing him, made her terror greater.

She heard her own breathing. And then she heard the scuff of leather on the floor in front of the bar, but she could not be sure just where it was.

This was by far the most nerve-shattering thing he had tried. She pictured herself paralyzed with fear if Tyner should leap up suddenly directly across the bar from her. She thought she might be so scared that she would stand helplessly while he lunged over the bar far enough to reach her.

Her eyes kept moving along the edge of the wood. She told herself she would be all right if she continued to keep her control. His trick was no good, it would not work. But the silence fought against her and threatened to break her nerves. Where was he? What was he doing?

She had to fight herself to keep from moving.

And then she saw him. She caught his reflection in the oval mirror of a dresser against the far wall. He was creeping toward her, coming toward the backside of the room. She went the other way, tiptoeing, but panic drove her as she came closer to the point where their lines of movement would be separated only by the bar.

She jumped and ran to get quickly past that point. Tyner heard her. She saw him grin and swing his head like a listening animal, and his face was the more frightening because she was seeing him when he thought he was unobserved.

Tyner swung around and started toward her again. She slipped her shoes off, and this time when she passed him just across the bar, watching him all the while in the dresser mirror, she forced herself to move slowly, noiselessly.

He crept on down to the front end of the bar and crouched there like a dangerous animal. Gail found the whistle. She blew it until her mouth was dry, pouring her desperation into the mouthpiece until she felt that her eyes were bursting.

That did not bring Tyner to his feet; he knew as well as she that Saber could not get in. What made him rise was the mirror. He was swinging to come back along the bar when he saw the mirror.

He and Gail stared at each other.

Tyner stood up, enraged because she had made a fool of him before he saw the mirror. His face was vicious with frustration. "You can throw the whistle away. If the cur ever got in here, I'd strangle him with my hands."

He leaned on the bar, and then he began to grin, as the looseness of his thinking, which had caused him to change so quickly from one attempt to another, now brought him a new idea. This time he had struck it.

He strode across the room and grabbed two heavy captain's chairs and threw them toward the front end of the bar. Carrying two more with him, he went to the end of the bar and blocked the passage between it and the wall, piling the chairs two-high, two-deep, laughing as he did so.

"Now! Now, by God, let's see you try to scoot around there again!"

Gail knew she was beaten. She had wasted time watching him use the chairs. She wasted no more, but ran to the woodbox and began to dig. It was too late. Tyner knocked the chairs and the tub over as he ran down the room, and the best Gail could do was swing around to face him with a stick of wood in her hand.

Tyner closed in grinning. She backed away.

FIFTEEN

Before he struck the floor of the basin, running in long downhill leaps, Bennion saw Durwood coming up the road. Bennion thought he heard a whistle blowing shrilly somewhere, faintly, far away, but he could not be sure because of the noise of his own running.

Instead of going straight down the street toward the Nose Paint, he made a detour into his camp and grabbed his carbine. He threw a shell into the barrel as he ran across the freight yard to squeeze between the fence and the assay office.

He let the hammer down to safety as he was crossing the street. The saloon door was still closed. He heard Tyner laugh.

When Bennion rammed the door open and went inside, he saw two overturned chairs near the stove and a tub of water still rocking on the floor as it spilled the last of its water from its corrugations. Gail was backing toward the storeroom door with an upraised stick of wood in her hand.

Tyner was moving toward her, slowly, deliberately.

Tyner swung around. Bennion had a good look at his expression and he had already seen Gail's face. There was no need of talk. Bennion's only problem for a moment was to keep from killing Tyner.

That wildness passed.

Tyner began to walk toward Bennion, with his hands patting the air. He staggered a little. "Take it easy, cowboy," he muttered. "No one's been hurt. There's no reason to get all—"

His drunkenness was not so marked when Gail's arm fell loosely and the stick of wood hit the floor with a loud thump. Tyner jumped and was all awareness in an instant, and that quick reaction made Bennion's anger start to rise again to the killing point.

Tyner kept coming. "I was a little drunk, see? I got so disgushted with this whole Chinese fire drill, I was a little drunk, see? She invited me in here. Thersh no reason to get all steamed up."

He was not drunk and Bennion knew it, and he knew that Tyner's cowardice, trapped as he was now, made him dangerous.

Bennion was about to step aside and motion Tyner toward the door, when a quick scrabble sounded on the porch. Something bounded into the room. A heavy body struck Bennion from behind and knocked him forward.

In a snarling fury Saber was slashing at him, ripping his clothes. Gail shouted at the dog.

Tyner grabbed the rifle barrel thrust so conveniently toward him. He jerked it hard and hauled Bennion in and tried to smash him in the face. More because of the unevenness of motion than by conscious effort, Bennion partly ducked the blow. It rocked along the side of his head and jarred him hard.

Gail was yelling at the dog, running toward him.

Bennion acted instinctively when he came against Tyner. He tried to grab Tyner's right wrist. He held on to the rifle with his other hand, and now the weapon was pressed between the two of them, lying across their bodies.

Bennion brought up his knee and rammed Tyner in the groin. He heard Tyner groan. The fire went out of him. Bennion wrenched the rifle loose. He started to bend the barrel over Tyner's head and then he saw there was no use.

Tyner's face was gray. He reeled against the wall and leaned there, holding his crossed hands low, nearly doubled. Saber was snarling as Gail held him. Bennion gave the dog a sour look, "There's a fine animal."

"He didn't know . . . He . . ." On hands and knees, Gail lowered her head and rested it against Saber's shoulder.

Bennion observed that she had no shoes. "You're all right, huh?"

She nodded without looking at him.

Bennion motioned Tyner outside. Durwood was coming up the street and Bennion was glad to see him.

"Down to the cabin," Bennion said, and Tyner obeyed, walking bent, with his hands still clasped low.

"I was drunk, see? She invited me in there. I'll swear she did. I'll swear on a stack of Bibles that's just what happened!"

Tyner did not try the lie on Durwood. He sat in a chair and looked sick when Bennion told Durwood what had happened.

"And that's over a woman," Durwood said, as if a woman were the merest trifle in the world. "Now you can understand the point of my little dissertation the other night."

"Let's forget the lectures right now. What do we do with Tyner?"

"Fifty years ago they would have hanged him, or beaten him half to death and thrown him out of camp. Maybe that's still sound punishment."

Tyner gave Durwood a look of terror, and Bennion watched Durwood sharply, wondering just how much the man believed what he was saying.

Durwood smiled at their reactions. "Tyner," he said, like a judge pronouncing sentence, "you've forfeited your right to stay in our little community. I think the best thing for you is to go down the river about as fast as you can walk." He looked at Bennion. "Agreed?"

Bennion nodded.

The declaration restored some of Tyner's

confidence. "I was going anyway. Anyone that wastes time here is a damn' fool."

"Fix a pack. Take what you need to reach the Bonnet," Durwood said.

"You're not stealing my rifle!"

"I'll give it to you, after we're a mile or two down the stream. Start packing, Tyner."

Tyner looked at his gear spread around the room. "You think I'm going to give all this stuff I packed in here to you guys, huh?"

"Bennion can take it out of here in time and send it to you." Durwood's voice went lower. "We don't feel like haggling, Tyner. We might lose patience and try the remedy I mentioned a moment ago."

Tyner looked quickly at Durwood and then at the floor. He just about believed Durwood, Bennion thought.

Tyner began to pack. He took three bottles of whiskey and some canned goods. He picked up his sleeping bag and threw it down. "Better take it," Durwood said.

From under the rail of Tyner's bunk, neatly wired out of sight between two small nails, Durwood retrieved the bolt of Tyner's rifle. Durwood smiled at the sullen look on Tyner's face when he saw the hiding place. "We'll leave the rifle unloaded," Durwood said. "I doubt that any bears will bother you between here and the Bonnet. You can make it by tomorrow afternoon,

I imagine, if you don't drown in the canyon."

Tyner was a beaten-looking figure when he was ready to leave. "My watch," he said, and went over to a table where it lay, fumbling aimlessly until Durwood picked up the watch and gave it to him. Tyner looked around the cabin as if there had been something here worth while and pleasant, something that he had not quite found through lack of trying.

There was a puzzled lostness in his eyes when he went outside. He looked toward the Nose Paint and muttered, "I don't know why I did that. So help me, I don't know . . ." When he looked at Bennion, hatred bubbled in his expression. "In a fair fight, I could tear you apart."

"There's no such thing as a fair fight," Durwood said cheerfully. "Shall we start?" Suddenly he noticed Bennion's ripped pants. "Say, that dog sort of got to you." He pulled aside a strip of cloth. "Jesus! He really did! You'd better dab something on those bites while I walk Tyner down the road."

Bennion watched them walk away, Durwood carrying the empty rifle and staying a few paces behind Tyner.

Pancake was close to town, tramping along unhurriedly. He stopped to talk a moment or two with Durwood when they met, and then he came on at a trot, his fishing rod cutting up and down and throwing flashes from its shiny surface. He was pink-faced and panting when he reached Bennion. "She's all right, ain't she?" he gasped.

"Sure," Bennion said.

"Sure! You damned young whelp! Stand there and say *sure* like you owned the world! After a woman's been scared like that you try talking to her or something. You don't stand around like a Bavarian outhouse and say *sure*. All you're thinking is what a great job you done running Tyner off. What do you think she's thinking right now?"

Bennion had never seen Pancake so perturbed. He followed the old man up to the Nose Paint. Saber came toward them and Gail said, "It's all right, Saber."

The dog sniffed Bennion's legs. "I ought to wrap this gun around your skull," Bennion said, but he knew that Saber, running toward the saloon when he heard the whistle, must have seen him running also, and that had been enough to excite the animal.

The tub was still upset. Gail had righted one of the chairs and was sitting on it and she had started to pick up the washing spilled across the floor, but she had got no farther than one piece which showed the mark of a footprint.

"Now it's all over, Gail," Pancake said soothingly. "It's all right, it's all right. Cry or cuss or do anything you want. It's all over."

Her face was still pale and tight. Then suddenly

the tenseness began to break. She stood up and leaned against Pancake and began to cry. "Go your best," he said. "That's the girl." He patted her on the back. His eyes were tenderly expressive, soft and hurt.

Bennion went back to his camp in the freight yard. He took off his torn pants and tried to see where Saber had bitten him. The dog had nailed him twice and one of the bites was deep and torn and bleeding freely. He could not remember feeling pain at the time. He found another wound, a long slash mark in his calf, and that one he could see to smear with antiseptic from his first-aid kit.

Some time later Pancake returned to camp. He hung his fish sack on the hub of a wagon wheel and said, "She'll be all right. Good, solid girl. I think she'd better sleep over here in one of the wagons tonight though. She'll rest better, being close to someone."

"You sound like an expert on women."

"Yeah? If you'd had the sense God gave geese in Ireland, you'd have kicked Tyner down the street and gone back to her and held her in your arms. You acted like a damn' fool, boy, not that you didn't get there and save her from being mauled."

Bennion was thinking along the same lines, so he did not argue or agree; he said nothing.

"All right," Pancake said, "stretch out there on

the wagon box. I'll see what I can do for your bites."

"I don't know. Considering the mood you're in—"

"Lay down!" Pancake said. He picked up the bottle of antiseptic and sniffed it. "What's this?"

"That's what I want you to use."

"Smells like swamp water," Pancake said, and threw the bottle away. "I got my own remedies.

"Hmn!" he said, in a professional tone, when he examined Bennion's wounds. "That one is a dandy. Guess I better wash my hands before I tackle that."

"I wouldn't get so scientific, doctor. What's a few more fish germs and cigar wrappers and—"

"Shut up." Pancake scrubbed his hands. He almost dried them on his shirt before he thought. "A good healthy dog bite never killed nobody, less'n it was rabies. Saber gets rabies shots regular. I asked her."

"Oh, he's a real healthy dog, all right. I could tell that from the way he clamped down."

"Hmmn," Pancake said. "Yep, I'll have to stitch that."

"Stitch it!"

"Lay still, I said! I got some nylon leaders, and if the hole don't get a bad infection or something, it'll probably be all right." Pancake began to mine in his gear.

"That's good," Bennion said, "that's real anti-septic."

"What do you think I carry around—bubonic plague?" Pancake came up with a heavy needle and a leader. He laid them on Bennion's back and then he got a cup of water and a small, dark bottle. "This iodine's a mite stout, so I'll cut it with water. Hold still."

Bennion felt the cold water trickling into the wound, and then the iodine hit and a moment later he stiffened out and hunched his back and said, "Cheerist!"

"Lay still! You only think that stings."

"Stings? It's burned a hole clear through."

Pancake threaded the needle. "This won't be expert of course, but—"

"After the way I've been treated so far, I wouldn't want an expert job. Hell no!"

"Shut up," Pancake said, and began to sew. "Good teeth that Saber's got, nice clean teeth, did you notice?"

"Yeah, I'm a great admirer of his teeth. Pancake, do you know what you're doing?"

"Sure I do. Hold still. This ain't hurting a bit."

"You got that much of a doctor's qualifications: *It doesn't hurt a bit.*"

Pancake grunted. He kept on stitching. After a while he said with pride in his voice, "You know that ain't a bad-looking job."

"I'll never see it."

"Hold steady now. I'm going to clip them stitches down with my fingernail clipper." Pancake did that. "Now a little bandage and some tape . . ." At last he said, "There you are, Johnny boy, the healthiest man you'll ever see with his ass in a sling." He began to laugh.

Bennion got up and put on a fresh pair of pants.

Pancake lit a cigar. "I told Gail we'd come over and eat with her. Keep her busy, you know. I left the fish with her. Guess we'd better invite Durwood too, and we'll all supply some grub."

"So you're not only a country doctor but a social director as well?"

"It's the best thing for her. People around and talking and all that. She said she didn't mind staying there in the saloon, but I know better. Something like that is a terrible shock, Johnny."

"Sure. You sound like it happened to you," Bennion said.

"That's real funny, boy. You didn't help by walking out after you busted Tyner."

"I had to do something with him," Bennion protested.

"Where'd you think he was going? You didn't have to spend an hour and a half having a trial over him. As far as that goes, you could've let Durwood handle him when he showed up." Pancake waved his hand. "You did what was natural, Johnny. It's just that I get all riled over something like that."

"Turn him over to Durwood, huh? I thought you didn't trust Durwood."

"I don't. Let's not howl any more about it. She's all right and Tyner's gone." Pancake picked up a tarpaulin and went over to a wagon. "This one will be close enough, but not too close." He climbed into the wagon and spread the tarp. "She's got a sleeping bag with an air mattress."

"What were you and Durwood getting so chummy about today?" Bennion asked.

Pancake stood in the wagon box, frowning. "We could rig a tarp over this, but I don't think it'll rain. Still . . . No, I guess we don't need it." He jumped down as easily as a boy. "Down there at the dams, you mean? Why, Durwood was trying to pump me about things I couldn't answer, same as you tried, Johnny. He was some slicker at it than you are, but he still wanted to know stuff that I don't know."

Pancake began to pick up gear around the camp. "Let's get this kind of straightened up. We don't want her to think we're living here like a bunch of Piutes."

"You want me to give Saber my sleeping bag?"

"You ain't funny." Pancake tasted the water in the bucket sitting on the all-purpose wagon box. "Phew!" he said, and spat it out. "That tastes like a Blackfoot Indian had been wading around in it. Get a fresh bucket, Johnny. She might want a drink in the night."

"I just got that bucket . . ." Bennion let it go, and went for a fresh bucketful of water.

Pancake was dumping cans in a sack. "You catch Durwood when he comes back and see to it he brings some grub too. I left her the fish but that ain't much, and we've been gobbling up her grub at an awful rate."

"Yes, general."

"I'll stay over there and help her cook."

"For a man that raised old Billy hell when he first saw a woman in 'our saloon,' you've sure changed your way of thinking, Pancake."

"A man that don't change his mind ten, twenty times a day is stupid as a frozen owl in a haunted outhouse," Pancake said, and started off with the sack. He began to sing "The Big Rock Candy Mountain," and Bennion grinned as he watched him go.

A half hour later when Bennion went to meet Durwood, he heard Pancake singing in the saloon. The old boy had a fair voice when he wanted to try. He was singing "Afton Water," not bawling it out as he often did his songs.

The old dead buildings, the feeling of lost time that was the mood of the town, caused Bennion to stop and listen, and he thought there was something crying, haunting, but still beautiful, in the way Pancake was singing.

And then he saw Durwood at the foot of the street.

They met at Durwood's quarters. "Any trouble?" Bennion asked.

"Oh, no. He growled because his rifle was empty when I gave it back, and he cursed you and said you'd steal everything he left here instead of sending it to him."

"Did he leave his address?"

Durwood gave Bennion a match folder with an address written inside the cover. "He'll get his gear," Bennion said.

Durwood poured drinks from one of the bottles Tyner had left. "I felt sorry for that poor bastard."

"How?"

Durwood shrugged. "Oh, just his complete lack of any sustained drive or objective. He's merely fumbling his way along, without grasping the meaning of anything. You know what he'll do now?"

"Sure. He'll go right on down the canyon and go home."

"That's exactly it." Durwood raised his glass. "After coming all the way here, with some pretty rough expenses for horses and the pack outfit, he spends part of one day actually on the glacier. Hardly worth the trip, was it?"

Durwood sat down. "Did you get your wounds patched up?"

"Pancake did some hemstitching of some sort."

"Remarkable old fellow. He really is. Who is he, Bennion?"

"I have no idea."

Durwood sipped his drink and blinked. "That means you're ruling out the possibility that he's your grandfather."

"I am."

"All I know about your grandfather is his name, so I'll take your decision. That makes our human skeleton a party unknown."

Bennion started to sit down and then thought better of it and stayed on his feet. "*Your* grandfather didn't throw in some facts on Pike that I don't know—something in his private letters?"

Durwood shook his head.

"He was mighty positive about him being in the glacier, without saying one more thing than just that."

"You're quite right. I've thought about the same thing many times. Frankly, Bennion, that unqualified statement, not the time prediction, which may be way off, was the clincher that brought me here." Durwood put his glass down and made a wry face. "I never could take whiskey straight."

"Nothing at all in Jackson's private letters?"

"Nothing on Pike that isn't known already. I've seen dark shadows all around that ancient robbery, and I've thought that my grandfather did too, but if he did, he never put one hint of suspicion down in writing. Unless he thought he could prove something, Stony Jackson didn't say it."

Bennion asked, "What kind of dark shadows are you talking about?"

"I think the Yankee Blade was being systematically looted by someone in the local management. That would have to be one of the Shores brothers. You ask why I'm guessing that and I'll tell you. In Jackson's papers there are copies of all the production and milling reports, and when you study them real close, you begin to wonder at the discrepancy between the final figures, the ounces of milled gold, and the tonnage estimates of ore blocked out in the mine. Somewhere in between, you begin to suspicion that someone was dipping with a big bucket."

Bennion said, "It could have been P. R. Shores. Gail says her family sort of thought so too."

Durwood sighed. "I'm glad to find my academic suspicions verified, but it doesn't help us now, does it?" He picked up the glass of whiskey and sniffed it and set it down. "So by now no doubt you've guessed that I've reversed my attitude of this afternoon. I'm staying on till we hang the last dog."

"What changed your mind?"

"That jackass Tyner dug up isn't our famous Whingding. There was no burro hair in the hole. That didn't strike me until I accidentally looked at Pancake's burro, and even then I wasn't sure that I knew enough about such matters to make a judgment.

"But this afternoon, down the river, that pale pink sand that's common to this stream attracted my attention and I found cupped rocks where the sand was encrusted as hard as cement in the hollows. I remembered that in some of those bone sockets of that burro skeleton I'd seen the same sand. There wasn't any sand like that in the hole Pancake started."

"I didn't notice the sand," Bennion said, "but I did give some thought to the lack of hair. I think you're right."

"Someone planted that burro skeleton," Durwood said. "Perhaps years ago, perhaps recently—within a few years, I mean."

"Pancake?"

"Who else?"

SIXTEEN

On September 11, one day before Stony Jackson's predicted time, Bennion and Durwood and Gail went out on the glacier about the *séracs* at Point 7. The windows they had cut so laboriously were now filled over.

In spite of previous summers on Hellsgrin, Bennion could not overcome a growing feeling of excitement. Today was as good as tomorrow. Jackson's calculation, believed or unbelieved, was still a powerful force to excite the mind.

"You stinker," Gail said, "Look at all the rocks you made me pile up over there to mark a phony line, when all the time it was hundreds of feet away."

"A hundred and thirty-seven feet," Durwood said. "Let's establish it again."

They walked up the glacier toward the ice fall. "I've got marks," Bennion said. "We won't have to climb up and find the original holes Jackson drilled. Those three-cornered holes."

"If you don't mind," Durwood said, "I'd like to sight it in again from the original points."

"Suit yourself."

They removed their light packs at the edge of the ice. Durwood set a Primus stove on a flat rock

233

surface, explaining, "Just so it won't get kicked around."

"Which side do you want to climb?" Bennion asked.

Durwood smiled. "Neither. I'll take your word. Where's your reference point on this side?"

That was not difficult to find; Bennion knew the rocks from memory and he found his own shallow drill hole in thirty seconds. Durwood stayed there while Bennion went across the glacier and found the other point. They signaled Gail in line between them and she marked the place with her jacket.

Once more with rocks they marked the line across the ice, this time the true line. The ice fall where Gail had toboganned on her stomach was about ninety feet ahead of the line.

Durwood pointed at it. "You say that's receded how far?"

"Between ninety and a hundred feet," Bennion said. "What did you make it from the pictures you used?"

"I had it less than that, but it was a guess. I'll take your figure, and you know what that means?" Durwood asked.

He always expected an answer. It was the teacher background, Bennion thought. "Sure, it means that Jackson's line was at the foot of the icefall in his day, or maybe a few feet into the icefall."

"Exactly," Durwood said.

His pedantic cocksureness was irritating, but Bennion was learning to accept it as part of the man, and he certainly had no lack of respect for Durwood's intelligence.

"At the risk of boring you by imposing personal observations, I would say that my grandfather selected this area of the glacier for several reasons. The obvious one is that it is the only place on the whole glacier where you can stand up.

"Number two, the ice is not as thick here as it is above and below this point. And three, it possibly was at one time clearer than in other portions of the glacier. Maybe it still is."

"Exactly," Bennion said.

They went on up to the icefall and this time Gail did not try to climb it. While Durwood and Bennion studied the frozen cascade, Gail walked off to the east where a thin sheet of water was running on the ice. It was about fifty feet wide at first, and then it gathered in a swale fifteen feet wide, and then it spread out again and followed the pitch of the glacier to the east and disappeared into the rocks.

"Why doesn't this ice melt?" Gail called. "The water is above freezing." Then she added, "Naturally."

"It comes from underground," Durwood said, "and its motion keeps it unfrozen, at least during the warm months."

"Give it another week," Bennion said. "It won't be running then."

Any thoughts about the weather carried urgency. If the usual pattern held, there would be a foot of snow in the high country by early October, and it was not at all unlikely that there would be snow long before then. In most places it would melt and beautiful weather would prevail until real winter came.

But the snow that fell on Hellsgrin would not melt.

"Well," Durwood said, "I suggest we start from right here and work out to both sides and down the ice until we strike the line."

"And then?" Bennion asked.

"We go on. And then, next summer, we come back and do it all over again, only hitting the places we missed before."

Bennion nodded. "It's as good as any way there is."

"Next summer I'll bring along a few aids, some kind of sonar rig and an ice scope."

"Sonar will keep us busy digging rocks all summer."

Durwood laughed. "We'll have the advantage of a short summer, at least. Right now it feels like winter is crouched just behind that isosceles rock over there." He pointed to a triangular rock beyond where Gail was dabbling in the water.

Once more they began the slow, uncertain task of cutting windows in the ice, following the same pattern they had used before, only this time they tried sprinkling dirt around the sloping edges of the holes. It did help kill surface reflection, they agreed.

Bennion tried his binoculars. He saw a splendid blur of nothing, no matter how he adjusted them. "I didn't think so," he said, "but . . ."

Gail tried an idea of her own. She emptied the lunch from her pack and curved the pack to form a shield part way around a window. That helped to improve the view and when Bennion got his pack and tied the two of them together to form a complete circle around the window, the idea was even better.

"We're real smart," Gail said. "Photographers were doing this about eighty years ago. Remember the black cloth they threw over their head?"

"All my baby pictures were taken that way," Bennion said, "eighty years ago."

"Skip shaving a few more days and I'll believe that."

Before noon they had worked a line of windows toward the west edge of the glacier. It was the same old story of seeing varying distances into the ice.

At one window, peering down past the canvas shield Durwood stiffened suddenly and leaned in closer, and then after a few moments he rose with a strange expression. "That gave me a start. Take a look."

Bennion knelt. It gave him a start too. Down there in the ice, like something floating free, was a huge rock that at first glimpse bore resemblance to the shape of a burro. He stood up. "How far would you say?"

"Six feet? It's hard to guess without digging."

Gail kneeled down to have a look, using her jacket to rest her knees on.

"I did dig a rock out once," Bennion said. "It was about seven feet deep and as I remember it appeared to be about as deep as this one does from the surface."

"That makes a good test case. I doubt that we'll be able to see anything much deeper than that. Next summer—" Durwood stopped and looked up as the sound of a light plane caught the attention of them all.

The plane came from the west, cutting so close to the Granite Mountains that Bennion knew the pilot was either an idiot or an experienced mountain flyer. He was the latter, Bennion decided a few moments later, when he saw how the pilot took advantage of the thermals and wind above the head of the glacier.

Someone in the plane saw them on the glacier, for the pilot banked and came directly overhead, rocking his wings as he passed on to the east. That just might be a search plane, Bennion thought, checking out some airline pilot's report of the wing on Black Bear Mesa.

"How long did it take?" Durwood asked.

"Take what?"

"To dig the rock out."

"Oh! The rock. I worked a couple of days at it, short working days, that is. I didn't actually dig it out, but worked down to it." Bennion kept listening to the sound of the plane.

He wondered what the ground party that would eventually reach the wrecked plane would think of Durwood's leaving the dying pilot. That is, if they were ever told about it. Actually, there was no reason why they should know.

In fact, the sharp edges of Durwood's behavior concerning the incident had worn down considerably. After knowing Durwood and understanding the uncluttered course of his mind, it was easier to accept his explanation, far easier than it had been at first. Yet the incident left a reservation every time Bennion thought of Durwood.

They resumed the job of making windows. Toward the western edge of Hellsgrin they encountered ice more static than the middle of the glacier, and there in a few places they could see down what seemed like a great distance, but it was likely no more than eight feet, both Durwood and Bennion estimated.

"You know," Durwood said, "I'm wondering

if the breaking of those granite shoulders that pinched the old icefall caused a change here. The rate of flow in the middle increased, and then let's say it almost stopped along the edges and there was a depression that filled with water.

"When it froze, the change was quiet and slow, and there was not so much cracking and disturbance, so now this ice is much clearer than out in the middle."

Durwood's theory seemed to be borne out when, near the very edge of the ice, they cut a window which opened vision far down the cold, sloping side of the gorge that contained the glacier. Small rocks were suspended down there like little fat fish swimming in misty blue water.

"There could be some measurable regularity involved here," Durwood mused. "It could be that a small body of water collects here, freezes, is crunched up and moved on, and then the cycle starts again. You've seen how ice floes pile up and heave, and then sink and—"

"I don't know about you two scientists," Gail called, "but I like to eat a little sometime near the middle of a working day, and that was an hour ago."

The plane returned while Durwood was digging a hole in the middle of the water sheet to fill the coffeepot. Gail and Bennion were over in the rocks, lighting the Primus stove.

They saw the aircraft only briefly. It roared

240

down across the break above the east end of the basin, showing for a few moments above the jagged rocks above the gorge, and then all but the engine sound was gone. Bennion kept listening until the sound was only a distant hum.

"He's drilling straight for some field, I'll bet. The chances are he's had a good look at the wreckage on Black Bear, and now he's headed straight for Bodley."

When Durwood came over with the coffeepot, he said, "Do you think he saw it?"

"I think so," Bennion said.

Durwood put the coffeepot on the stove. "How long will it take, the report, organizing a search party—the whole business of getting to the plane?"

"The organization doesn't take long because it already exists. It's just a matter of getting the men together. If they start from Randall, two days will do it. From Bodley, it's about the same, because they'll know over there about the road Gail used. Why?"

"Why? Because I'll want to meet the party and explain what happened," Durwood said. "I don't want to be the cause of an all-out search for a survivor. Who makes up those search parties?"

"Men who know the area," Bennion said. "They might be anybody. The sheriff, or one of his deputies, generally leads them."

"Not that deputy I saw?" Gail said.

241

Bennion laughed. "Not him, no!"

If the sheriff was back from his vacation and led the search party, Bennion had no doubt that he would continue as far as Basin City. The tracks of Bennion's horse near the plane would make him wonder, and then of course he would have the reports from the pilot who had seen three people on Hellsgrin.

"If they come in from Randall, from the east, we won't even know about it," Bennion said. "They'll go to the plane and that will be it." He wondered how much of that Durwood would swallow.

"I've been thinking about that," Durwood said. "I'll give them two days and then I'll go over to the plane. If no one shows up, I'll leave a note telling them where I am."

Would he? Maybe he would, at that, Bennion thought.

The sun left the glacier while they were eating lunch, and with its going time seemed to jump ahead five hours. Gail put on her jacket. "I see what you mean about winter being just around the corner."

"Freezing could start here any time," Bennion said.

Durwood looked out at the water sheet. "That might help, because we're not going to do any good here until we do something about the water."

"We can ditch it away, clear from this side of the icefall," Bennion said.

They worked for three more hours, avoiding the area covered by water. Durwood had set the pattern of the grid their windows made, pacing five steps between each cut. They all recognized the serious flaw of that spacing. Thorough coverage would have meant cutting the windows no more than five feet apart.

There was not time for such coverage. It would take thirty-five hundred windows, Durwood figured, to cover at the present spacing the whole area between the field of *séracs* and the icefall. At the rate they had gone so far, it would require a month to cover the workable field, and before that time there would be snow on the glacier.

Durwood was limping when he walked over to put on his pack. His bad knee had not taken kindly to the kneeling at the windows. "I'll bring some paper tomorrow and make a plat of what we've done. We don't want to be cutting holes in the same places next year."

Next year. He was right, Bennion thought. It could be then, or four years away, or never. He remembered the ice on the west side of the glacier. It was almost stagnant there. An unusually long warm cycle would affect Hellsgrin greatly, for the life of the glacier depended on vast accumulations of snow.

There were so many factors . . . Jackson

undoubtedly was aware of them all, but how could he have predicted long-range weather. Meteorological data on this tiny local area of the mountains had been lacking in his time; it was still lacking. The often encountered statement of old-timers that the basin was "a hell of a place for snow thirteen months out of the year" was hardly scientific.

Gail said, "Get your whip, Canute." And it was then that Bennion realized he had been glaring at the glacier as if it were a personal, living enemy.

They were on the outfall in warm sunshine, going, down toward Basin City, when Durwood said, "Have you ever tried looking into the ice at night, Bennion?"

"A half-dozen different ways."

"No good, huh?"

"A gaslight was no good at all, even inside a tent. A long beam flashlight was better, but mostly it threw everything back in your eyes."

"How about colored light?" Durwood asked.

"I tried red. No good."

"I see. I've got a light with blue, red, and green discs over the lens. You want to come up here some night with me and try them all?"

"No. I don't think any color will help."

"Maybe not." Durwood said, "but I might give it a go. This is the eleventh. At least by next Tuesday, I've got to be on my way back to work, so I'm ready to try anything."

"Suppose the weather holds good and we stay on and find the gold after you've left?" Gail asked.

Durwood smiled. "That would be strictly up to you people then to decide whether or not I've been any use, and whether you cared to give me at least a bar as a memento of the occasion. However, if anyone is willing to bet, I've got a month's salary that says we'll be here next year."

"I suspect you make too much money, and I'm beginning to appreciate that glacier," Gail said, "so you get no bet from me."

"Let me pick my month and I'll make the bet," Bennion said.

Pancake was sitting on the Nose Paint steps, with Gail's file of the *Basin Advocate*. Saber was sprawled out at his feet. The old man was wearing glasses, which he put away hastily when he saw the three people at the head of the street.

"Got your knees wet again, I see," Pancake said.

"Guess how many burros we found today," Bennion said.

Pancake snorted. "Hah! Give me something hard to figure out." To Gail he said, "I've got a big stew going. It'll be ready in about an hour."

They all ate together in the Nose Paint. Afterward, Durwood borrowed Gail's rod and went down the creek. Bennion and Gail and Pancake were playing pinochle when Durwood returned after dark, with a mess of native trout that made Pancake's eyes pop.

"Yeah, sure," Pancake said. "Anybody can catch fish like that if he wants to use big flies after dark and take a chance on drowning in one of them holes and fumbles around in the willows half the night. Sure, you can catch fish that way."

Pancake was still in a grumpy mood when he and Bennion went to their camp.

"I'll bet you found that old newspaper file interesting," Bennion said.

"A pack of damn' lies about everything! That editor never got nothing right in all his life. Reading his stuff today made him an even bigger liar than he was when he wrote it. He was a drunken bum that had to make a living washing dishes in a Chinese whorehouse after he left here, and then he died of the horrors behind a salmon canning factory."

Bennion had to laugh, and after he was in bed he thought of the statement again and chuckled, and Pancake told him irritably that a man ought to have better manners than to keep everybody in camp awake all night with senseless heehawing.

SEVENTEEN

Jackson's prediction was still the guide on which they based their work on the glacier, but it had lost all its power to excite. This was the day, but when the hour and minute came, only Gail remembered. She looked at her watch and glanced down the ice to where the rock monuments marked the line, and then she went back to work smoothing with the sharp hoe the cuts Bennion made with the ice plane.

The time passed and it made no more impression here than the ticking of millions of other seconds during the preceding fifty years.

Gail looked at the dark rocks above her, at the tumbled ice up the gorge, at the wild field of *séracs* where the crevasses ran in crazy patterns. It was hard to think that anything ever changed here, or that anything ever would. And if Hellsgrin had a secret, Hellsgrin was not obliged by the mathematics of anyone to reveal that secret.

Its blue-white depths were inviolate, its traditions all its own, its history unknown and forever to be unknown.

She could not glare at it as Bennion had the day before, wanting to rip it apart by force; nor could she curse it sullenly as Tyner had done, like a primitive man growling his resentment and fear of elements not understood as he dogtrotted to shelter in a cave.

Durwood's view of the glacier was different too. Gail knew he did not regard it as an enemy, or as a great unknown to be feared, but as a problem that could be solved by no great display of human force, but rather by the ingenuity of scientific instruments that he would bring to bear upon it when he returned next summer.

Gail merely accepted Hellsgrin. She remembered standing on the Monte Rosa in Switzerland, with her mind reaching across the world to Hellsgrin, and she had been shocked and awed by the view. And afterward, the Swiss innkeeper in Gornergrat had said, "The Monte Rosa? It is there. It is part of us. What is there to say about it?"

That was the answer. Hellsgrin was a part of them, she and Durwood and most of all, Bennion.

She watched the little dam they had built where the diversion ditch in the ice crossed a low spot. She and Bennion had carried the dirt in buckets for a long distance while Durwood was picking out the ditch.

It was going to hold, that tiny earthen dam. A little lake had grown behind it, raising the water level so that it flowed away in the connecting ditch that ran into a crevice in the rocks on the east side of the glacier.

The tiny stream flowing in its icy channel, so small that a man could have blocked it with his hand, was part of the flow that came booming from under the glacier at the final icefall, part of the Sorrowful River.

Gail dabbled in it with her hoe, for a moment caring nothing about gold or ancient mysteries.

"You getting tired, doll baby?" Durwood asked, grinning.

"Don't ever call me that!"

Durwood sobered instantly. "I'm sorry. I really am." He called to Bennion, "Shall we call it a day?"

"Deep enough for me," Bennion said, and put his ice plane down.

That evening after dinner Durwood said, "I'm going to rest until dark and then go up with my colored flashlight. You want to come with me, Bennion?"

"I'd rather play pinochle."

"I know what you're thinking," Durwood said, "but I'm going to be foolish anyway. Tomorrow, I've got to go over to the plane, and then in two days more I've got to leave, so I'd better exhaust my little theory while I can."

After he was gone, Gail said, "Do you think he really will go all the way to the plane?"

"Yes," Bennion said.

"Hah!" Pancake snorted.

"Why not?" Gail asked.

"Because you just can't believe nothing he says. He's a truth-telling liar and them's the worst."

"That's Pancake's special kind of liar," Bennion explained, "one that overwhelms you with the truth until you can't believe anything he says."

"Up to a point." Pancake waggled his finger. "And then he sticks a knife in your back. Now you take me, I mix the whoppers in with a little truth, so nobody that don't know me well can figure what I'm saying."

"That's a fact," Bennion said.

"Jim Bridger, he had a different way of lying," Pancake went on. "He sized up his audience and if he was telling a story about wrassling a grizzly bear in mortal combat and seen that people was damn' fool enough to believe any man would wrassle a bear, then he threw in a couple, three more grizzlies to make it all the more interesting."

There was nothing Pancake liked better than an audience. He lit a cigar and lectured for some time on different methods of lying, until both Gail and Bennion were laughing. But in the end he went back to Durwood. "He'll tell you what you already know, and maybe something more that you're guessing at, and by that time you're saying, 'Now there's a real honest man,' and about then he steals all the chips and walks away."

"You really think so?" Gail asked seriously.

"I know it. What's he doing up there on Hellsgrin at night?"

"Wasting time," Bennion said, "the same as I have a good many nights."

"Hah! Durwood never wasted no time in all his life. His brain is working even when he's asleep."

"He can't steal the glacier," Bennion said.

"No, but he could see something down in one on them holes you've been cutting, and you think he'd tell you about it if he did?"

Gail said, "I didn't think you believed there was anything to see up there, Pancake."

"I don't! I said *if* he saw something." Pancake sighed. "I just may have to go up there and set around with your carbine, Johnny, and keep an eye on things."

"Why?" Bennion said. "If we don't find anything, Durwood has no reason to try a shenanigan, and you're convinced that there's nothing to find."

Pancake slid out of that trap by saying, "I was just trying to show you that you can't trust everybody you meet. Hell, I ain't going to waste my time up there getting rheumatism sitting on a cold rock."

Gail and Bennion looked at each other quietly. "One honest question and answer, Pancake. We know you're not L. G. Riddle, because he was a crackpot. You know all about him, sure enough, but you're not him. Who are you?"

"I'm Bloody Bill," Pancake said, "one of the robbers that took the mill gold. We had to leave it here when we skipped because we were under suspicion. There was three of us, but Meathead Jones was the only one that knowed where the loot was hid.

"That was on account of him being the leader and he one that cased the heist, and besides, when he was just a little scaper, his ma told him never to trust anybody he robbed a mill with. We were all coming back together to get the gold when the heat was off, but Meathead he got killed when a church roof collapsed on him, and Blue Belly Buster died not a month later from drinking too much lemonade on a hot day at a Sunday school picnic.

"That left me the only living robber, but not knowing where the stuff was stashed, I been looking and seeking all these years, and it looks like I'll have to keep it up for a long time yet." Pancake leaned back and puffed smoke at the ceiling. "The whole truth, so help me Finnegan. I think the gold is in an old crosscut on the third level of the Yankee. We can get it just as soon as we raise a hundred thousand dollars to open up the tunnel again."

Gail and Bennion looked at each other helplessly.

"And you're the one who called the editor a liar," Bennion said.

"Yep!" Pancake grinned. "Now let's go to bed so's you can dream up some more silly questions."

"You should have left just before you told that story, Pancake," Gail said. "Not that I don't believe every word of it."

Gail and Bennion were making a shield of heavy wire and canvas to use at the windows in place of the packs, when Durwood came by on his way to the plane.

"Did you do any good last night?" Bennion asked.

"No. But by next summer I'll do some research on different light qualities and I'll bet I'll have something to penetrate at least deeper than we've been able to do so far." Durwood looked toward the east. "You think two days is enough time for a search party to reach the plane?"

"If the plane we saw made the report, and if a ground party started right away."

Durwood nodded. "If they come from the west, they'll have to pass through here. Tell them where the plane is, Pancake, and tell them I'm waiting there."

"Yeah," Pancake said. He watched Durwood sourly as the man went up the street and started to climb on the outfall. "Tell me his conscience is bothering him, why don't you?"

"Not his conscience," Bennion said. "He's merely following out logical procedure. He knows what a mess of unnecessary trouble there'll be if someone finds that plane, not knowing what happened to him."

"I know what should have happened to him," Pancake growled.

"Just exactly what have you got against Durwood?" Gail asked.

"He's no good, that's all," Pancake said, and walked away.

After the first few cuts they made in the area where the water had run, Gail and Bennion knew that this part of the glacier was somewhat like the western edge where the ice had been uncommonly clear. Bennion wondered if they were wasting time exploring the edges of the ice.

They argued about that point, but in the end they agreed that the best plan was to maintain their grid.

"I love patterns and plans," Bennion said. "They're always so logical. When I was a kid, I remember an old fellow who told me the way to find something lost was to start walking in a circle, gradually closing in until you found whatever you were looking for."

"Right in the middle of the big circle?"

"No. I never started the circle big enough and whatever it was that I'd lost was always clear outside of it, and if I ever found it, it was by stumbling over it accidentally when I was looking for something else I'd lost."

Gail said, "I gather that you lost practically everything you got your little paws on, so naturally you had a chance of finding something no matter where you looked."

The surface of the ice where the water had flowed was faintly yellow. Its roughness smoothed away easily under the ice plane. They completed the first grid line to the eastern edge of the glacier and then, fifteen feet away, started another row of windows running west.

The shield they had made that morning proved its usefulness. By the use of their hands beside their faces and by raising or lowering their faces, they could regulate the amount of light striking the surface of the ice.

On the fourth window they cut from the eastern edge of the glacier, almost in the middle of the swale where the water had run, Gail spent more time than usual, twisting and turning her head as she looked into the ice.

"A rock?" Bennion asked.

"Probably. I'm looking obliquely, actually looking under it, I think. See what you make of it."

When Bennion's eyes adjusted he saw what she meant. He was not seeing the object, but, rather, the blur of its shadow. Whatever it was that threw the shadow was farther down the swale and much closer to the surface.

They cut another window, guessing at the

position of the object. There they struck opaque ice and could not see in any direction more than a few inches.

Bennion studied the slant of the sun, which had a short time yet to lie on the glacier. "I think we overshot because of the angle of the light coming into that first hole."

"Let's not outguess ourselves," Gail said. "Let's just cut holes until we hit the right place." She walked forward two paces. "How about here?"

"A beautiful mathematical calculation! Let's dig."

Two light planes went over, flying east, while they were making the window. Bennion said, "Durwood is likely to have company over there, sure enough. Those planes are probably in contact with a ground party."

Gail smoothed the hole with the hoe and Bennion set the shield over it. He was still thinking about the planes when he kneeled down.

For an instant there was no belief; it was unreal. He was deluding himself, and then the fact seeped through and could not be denied. He was looking straight down into the face of a man, a man embedded in the cold blueness, with one arm reaching out above his head, and with his legs all strangely twisted.

Bennion stood up quickly. It was like coming back from the frozen depths. Gail looked at his face and said nothing. Bennion nodded, pointing toward the shield.

Gail knelt to look and then she hesitated and turned her head toward Bennion.

"A man," he said.

She hesitated longer before she lowered her head above the shield. When she rose, there was a strange, shocked look in her eyes. "That's— that's incredible."

They took turns looking and the first startling impact began to diminish and they gathered facts from the frozen figure. He was dressed in heavy clothes, high boots with overshoes on top of them, and a sheepskin coat.

His face—it could have been the distortion of the view through the ice—appeared misshapen. The left hand on the arm that was extended bothered Bennion most of all, for he could see the fingers hooked out like talons, and they spoke of the last instants of life, of a clawing and grasping at snow plunging into the bergschrund.

"What can you tell?" Gail asked.

Bennion shook his head. The man was buried no more than four feet deep, but Bennion did not want to dig him out, not yet, not until there was a place to bury him as soon as possible after he came from the frozen clutch of the glacier.

"Let's go get Pancake," he said.

"To help dig the ice?"

"No. Just to look." Bennion started away.

"There's no need for you to walk all the way down there and back."

"I'd rather."

They did not speak of the burro, or any possibilities of finding it, on the way to Basin City.

Pancake was washing the front window of the Nose Paint. He saw them coming and sat down on the porch.

"We want you to go up to the glacier with us, Pancake," Bennion said. "We found a man in the ice."

Pancake opened and closed his mouth without speaking, and then he said, "I don't believe it."

"Yes," Gail said, "we found a man."

Pancake shook his head slowly. "All right. Let's go."

Up on Hellsgrin, after Pancake stood up from peering into the ice, he kept wagging his head. "Good Lord, good Lord! Would you believe it!" he mumbled.

Gail and Bennion glanced at each other, and then they stared at Pancake, waiting for him to go on.

"So that's where he ended up?" Pancake murmured. "After all these years . . ." He turned suddenly and looked at Bennion. "Dealer Dan. I'd know him through twenty feet of ice."

"Dealer Dan!"

"Sure as shooting. I never knew a man who had feet as cold as his. He always wore overshoes on top of his boots, and never went twenty feet outside without that heavy sheepskin. Besides that, I know his face."

Gail and Bennion kept watching Pancake.

"And he always took along a burro with a pack-saddle and heavy leather panniers, wherever he went," Bennion said. He pointed at random at another window. "That burro over there."

The bluff did not move Pancake one inch. "When you find a burro, Johnny boy, I'll put in with you, and then I'll eat the burro, hair, hide and all."

"All right," Bennion said, "how did Dealer Dan get in the glacier?"

"How would I know? I always thought he skipped town, and so did everyone else."

"You're honestly sure this *is* Powell?" Gail asked.

Pancake scuffed at the ice with his boot. "Yep! I always heard he went to Arizona, and later to Los Angeles and made a fortune, but all that time here he was in the ice." Pancake clucked his tongue. "And him a man that hated having cold feet."

"Why would anyone kill him?" Bennion asked.

"Hah! There were husbands in Basin City that had plenty of reason to kill him. Another thing, he always carried gold on him, and that would be enough reason for some men to knock him over and dump him in Hellsgrin."

"Gold pieces?" Bennion said.

"Sure. He"—Pancake's hesitation was very slight—"was like a lot of other tinhorn gamblers."

"Gold pieces in a leather purse?" Gail said.

"Loose, or in a purse, or someway—I ain't got no idea about that." Pancake shuffled his feet. "I'm getting off this ice before I break something."

"Just a minute," Bennion said. "You told me once that Dealer Dan wouldn't have been caught dead in overalls, but here we find a man roughly dressed and you swear it's Dealer Dan. How—"

"He ain't wearing overalls. Anyway, during the winter in Basin City most anyone was likely to be rough dressed in whatever was warm." Pancake started away. "I'm getting tired of your crazy questions, Johnny."

Bennion put out his arm but he did not touch Pancake. "Just a minute. I'm going to tell you where Dealer Dan Powell really is, as if you didn't know. He's down there in that wooden box beside the trench, beside the skeleton of the burro you dug up from somewhere along the river and planted for us to find, right along with an old packsaddle you found somewhere."

"Is that a fact?" Pancake sighed and wagged his head. "You can sure dream up some dandies, Johnny. Now I'll tell you what I'm going to do, I'm going to risk my neck again getting down from this cotton-picking place and I'm going to dig a hole in the old cemetery, so's when we take

Dealer Dan out of here we can plant him before he stinks up the town worse than he did when he was alive."

Pancake walked off the ice and began to pick his way through the rocks.

"And there you are," Gail said.

"Yep! That was a real fact-finding session. I wonder what we could get out of him if we heated .30-30 shells red hot and put 'em between his toes?"

"He'd tell you a story about smuggling diamonds out of South Africa, Johnny boy."

Bennion took another look into the ice. He peered a long time at the clutching hand, until he experienced the eerie feeling that the hand was opening and closing at the same rate he was breathing.

He could not tell whether or not there was a golden band on the ring finger.

They both had enough for one day. On their way to get the packs, Gail said, "It's foolish, I know, but I keep thinking the ice will make some big cracking lurch, or something, and then we won't be able to find the place tomorrow."

"Me too."

They looked out at the ice as they put on their packs. The window was about twelve feet north of the fourth hole in the second row below the icefall, a window all by itself, and there were only four windows in the second row.

261

It was impossible that they would forget, or that the glacier could hide what they had found. During the next twenty-four hours, from one end of two miles of ice to the other, there would be only six inches of movement.

But before they left, they piled rocks around the window and left one of the ice planes sticking upright in the middle of the marker.

Pancake was digging on the hill north of town, and Saber was there, giving his usual assistance. Gail and Bennion did not go up to the old cemetery and Pancake stayed there until well after sunset. By then Durwood had returned.

"No one there," he said. "Two planes circled the mesa and I waved at them. I left a note and they can come to me now."

Bennion told him about the man in the glacier, and Durwood's first question was, "How far from my grandfather's line?"

"Short by fifty or sixty feet."

"That's amazing!"

"If it's Alonzo Pike," Bennion said.

"Oh, you don't know yet?"

"Pancake swears it's a gambler who disappeared the year before the robbery."

"During the winter?"

Bennion nodded.

Durwood looked over toward the toe of the mountain where Pancake had dug the trench.

"Yeah," Bennion said. "We think so too."

"What's Pancake doing up on the hill now?"

"Digging a grave."

"I'll be a monkey's uncle! He spends all his time either digging them up or preparing to plant them!"

EIGHTEEN

The next morning Pancake suggested to Bennion that they use dynamite to free the body from the ice, and Bennion rejected the idea instantly.

"Take your gun," Pancake said.

"No. What for?"

"If you don't know by now, I can't convince you."

"We haven't found any gold, Pancake. We're not going to find any, remember?"

"I ought not bother to help you," Pancake grunted, "and maybe I just won't."

But he went along.

The ice plane had fallen over, but the rocks were still there and the window was still there and after they smoothed the surface of it again, Bennion saw that the body was still there also.

Durwood took a look and rose chewing his lip. "That's Dealer Dan, Pancake?"

"Dig him out! I'll prove it."

Durwood gave Bennion a startled look. "I think he means it."

You could not tell from looking at the old man. He could be playing a bluff to the last gasp, or telling the truth, or getting ready to pull something out of his sleeve that would be a mixture of truth and bluff. "Dig him out! We'll see!"

Durwood said, "You can identify your grandfather, Bennion?"

"Maybe."

"That *maybe* is just what Pancake will hit us over the head with."

"I'll do the digging," Bennion said. "The rest of you can look for Whingding. If he's here, he should be close."

Gail and Durwood began to cut more windows. Pancake went over in the rocks and sat by a fire built from wood he had packed up on his back.

With the handle of one of the ice planes, Bennion measured carefully. He made reference points with rocks beyond the area where he intended to dig, and then he went to work with a pick and an ax. He kept the sides of the excavation straight and the center low and shoveled the white spalls away when they collected in the low spot.

It was awkward footing until Gail brought him a piece of canvas to stand on. He worked with deliberate purpose, popping the ice chips loose from the sides with the ax, making slower progress with the pick as he carried the middle low, shifting the canvas from one end of the hole to the other.

When the spalls began to grow into a glittering embankment around the hole, Pancake could stand his isolation no longer. He came across the ice. The excavation was then about two feet deep. "Hey, hey!" Pancake muttered. "Easy with that pick, boy."

"I thought you hated Dealer Dan."

"I did," Pancake said quietly. "God! How I did." Pancake's warning was timely. A spall popped free from a pickstroke and exposed the thumb of the man's hand, and that was no more than thirty inches from the surface. Carefully, as if there were still live nerves in the tortured hand, Bennion picked away the encasing ice.

There was a wide gold band on the ring finger.

Bennion stopped and looked up at Pancake.

"No," the old man said, "no, that's not Dan."

Durwood and Gail came over to the hole. Bennion reached down and touched the ring. He knew how cold and solid the feel of the hand would be, and still it shocked him. He drew away, staring down at it.

Durwood poised the ice plane. He jabbed with it, hard and deftly and the two middle fingers of the hand snapped off. They looked at him in horror.

"That's what you were debating about, wasn't it, Bennion? How to get the ring off."

The ring was easily recovered then. The coldness of it seemed to burn Bennion's hand as the warmth of his flesh melted away the last of the ice that had imprisoned it for half a century.

Gail flipped a piece of crumpled yellow tissue from her shirt pocket and tossed it to Bennion.

He wiped the ring carefully. It was engraved inside the band.

His grandparents' first names. Their wedding date.

He put the ring in his pocket and got out of the hole.

"Pike?" Durwood asked.

Bennion nodded. "I'll finish the job later, when I've decided where to bury him and made arrangements."

Gail put her hand on his shoulder lightly and then she walked away and went back to work with Durwood. Pancake turned away suddenly and went over to his tiny fire.

"The burro has to be here," Durwood said. "Let's keep expanding the circle."

Once more Bennion tried to get something from Pancake. "Even now, haven't you got anything to say?"

"No. I didn't think he was there. I'm all mixed up now. What do you expect me to say?"

It was futile. Bennion tried, but Pancake said he knew no more than anyone else. "I always held he never went in the glacier. Now I'm wrong, so that makes me worse off for facts than the rest of you."

Gail made the next discovery ten minutes later. She was looking into the canvas shield when she gave a small cry and stood up so hastily that she knocked the shield sliding on the ice.

They took turns at the window. Down in the soft blue gloom they saw the hindquarters of a burro. The breeching strap was still in place around the rump and under the tail, and the leather had been cut in the same hard straight line of shearing that had separated the hindquarters of the animal from the rest of the body.

At some point in Hellsgrin, the ice had strained and cracked and broken the burro in two more neatly than if it had been cut with a giant saw.

"That's not quite the part we want," Durwood said matter-of-factly. "It creates an area for the introduction of rough humor, but I sense we're not in the mood for it."

He found Whingding after cutting four more windows close together. The back of the burro was closer to the surface than the body of the man, and they could see the leather panniers still on the tipped packsaddle.

Whingding was tilted in the ice, so that they had a side view. The head and the position of the front legs gave the illusion that he was walking through the ice, but the terrible clopped-off flatness behind the saddle did not let the illusion live for more than an instant.

The burro lay up the glacier from where Pike was, both of them under the dip of the ice where the water had been running.

Pancake stood with his hands in his pockets and watched them work. The only help he gave was when he handed Bennion the ax, with a warning look that said, *Keep your hands on it.*

Bennion chopped and used the pick and Durwood shoveled out the spalls. Gail went over to the fire and made coffee, and even though she brought it out on the ice, no one but Pancake had time to drink a cup of it. She took the cups and pot back to the fire, and then she watched the digging.

They reached the pannier that was closer to the surface. It came apart like the ice, in brittle chips. The golden bars were there, small and very heavy. One by one Bennion and Durwood hacked them free and tossed them up to Gail, who whacked the rest of the ice from them.

There were five of them in the pannier. Everyone but Pancake felt and hefted them and made his own calculations.

"Seventeen pounds each?" Durwood said.

"About fifteen," Bennion said. He saw Pancake nod.

"All right, that's seventy-five pounds." Durwood chewed his lip nervously. "That figures a hundred and fifty pounds of gold, instead of three hundred, providing the other pannier has the same number of bars."

"It does," Pancake said quietly, and before anyone could make anything of that, he added, "You always put the same weight on both sides of a pack."

Yes, Pancake, Bennion thought, *but you slipped before a couple of times and mentioned fifty thousand dollars, when all reports said at least ninety thousand dollars.* And fifty thousand would be quite close to the accurate figure.

Bennion began to chop again, working toward the other pannier. He and Durwood hacked their way down to it and pried the gold from the ice. Five more bars.

"I wonder why they made them so small," Gail said.

"Cute." Pancake held one of the pigs a moment and then dropped it and kicked it back toward the other bars when it slid on the ice. "Cute and dangerous."

Durwood hauled himself out of the hole and dropped the shovel. "It looks like there may be one more in that pannier, but I'm going to have a cup of coffee before I dig another inch." He walked toward the rocks.

Bennion pulled the shovel to him and cleaned out the spalls. He got down on his hands and knees to see if he could spot another bar. Gail squatted at the edge of the excavation and held the pick.

"I don't see anything that looks like a bar, unless—" Bennion said, and it was then that Pancake took them both by surprise.

Pancake gave Gail a violent shove and knocked her into the hole on top of Bennion. As he struggled to get up, Bennion thought, *I didn't think he'd try anything.* An instant later Pancake's weight struck them as the old man piled into the hole, and at the same time the rifleshot made crashing echoes against the dark rocks.

"Stay down!" Pancake yelled. "He's got Tyner's rifle!"

They were piled and tangled like a litter of wrestling kittens. Pancake shoved Gail down again when he thought her head was showing above the hole. "Keep down!" He pulled a pistol from his bulky coat and shoved it butt first at Bennion. "He caught me short. I let him get away with it."

It was Gail's pistol.

Bennion crawled and slid across the hole and raised his head slowly, looking through a low spot in the pile of spalls. He located Durwood's position. About fifteen feet up in the rocks behind the packs.

Durwood located him also. The rifle bullet smashed into the spalls and cut Bennion's face with bits of flying ice. Bennion sat down quickly.

Tyner's rifle. Sure. Durwood had not given it back to Tyner; he had hidden it after sending Tyner on his way. Then that night he had fished after dark, he had picked it up and brought it to town. And then all that fine, convincing talk about trying out his light theory after dark on the glacier.

"He stalled over there at the coffeepot," Pancake said. "He almost fooled me. Then the next time I looked, he was up in the rocks. I saw a piece of canvas go flying, and he swung the rifle around."

Bennion checked the pistol. It was good for a standoff only. Durwood was no more than a hundred and fifty feet away and behind the rocks. He had the bulge. The more Bennion's mind raced over the fix, the less chance he saw for any of them to get clear. "This is all the shells?"

"Hell yes," Pancake said. "After I found it in the woodbox, all I figured I'd need was one or two to kill him at close range if he started something. Can you hit him?"

"Maybe." Bennion did not give himself an outsize chance of scoring with the pistol, unless Durwood came out of the rocks. "If we don't let him know we have it, he may come down out of there."

"No!" Pancake said. "He'll hold out."

"Then *we'll* have to," Gail said. She was huddled in a corner of the hole, her eyes big and frightened.

Pancake leaned over and patted her knee. "We're going to get out of this, don't you worry."

I'd like to know how, Bennion thought. Up there in the rocks, Durwood could jump around and pound himself and exercise and keep warm, but in this rough, icy hole there was not room to swing a cat. In two hours they would be so chilled, it would be difficult to move swiftly.

By night, when there would be some chance of popping out of the trap and scattering in different directions, they would be so stiff from cold that no one of them would have more than a wild chance of getting away from the rifle shots that would rock across the ice.

Bennion took off his shirt and undershirt. He slipped the T-shirt over his head, drawing it down to his eyebrows. He raised his head slowly. He spotted the rifle. It was tipped up slightly, resting in the split of two rocks. He knew it had a scope and that some men cannot use a scope quickly on running shots, or even accurately.

While he was trying to make something of those facts, the rifle moved. He fell back in the hole as a bullet chipped the edge of the ice where his head had been.

"We'll *have* to wait him out," Gail said. "It will be just as hard on his nerves as ours."

"He hasn't got any," Pancake muttered. "Can't you get a shot at him, Johnny?"

"I will, before it's over." Bennion had sweated from the digging. As he put his shirt on, he thought of his down jacket lying over there in the rocks. He wondered if he could cut out a block of ice big enough to protect him while he slid it toward the rocks.

It was only an idea. There was no room to work

in the hole, and the ax was out beyond the pile of spalls.

"Let him have the gold," Gail said. "Tell him he can have it if he lets us walk away."

"No!" Pancake said. "If he'd had any thoughts of that, he wouldn't have fired that first shot without warning. If he lets us go, he's burdened down with a hundred and fifty pounds of weight, and he knows Sam Harding won't pack for him. He's got to have his own sweet time to get away, and he can't do it if he leaves us alive. Durwood had his mind made up when he cached that rifle."

Without moving from where he was, Bennion shouted, "Durwood! Durwood! You can have the bars. All we want is to get out of here."

They waited, looking at each other.

There was no answer.

Pancake tried a cautious peek, ducking back quickly. His eyes rolled shrewdly as he put his hat on the blade of the shovel. He raised the shovel inch by inch, pulling it down twice during the process, simulating the action of a man poking his head up nervously.

A bullet took the rib of the blade and knocked the tool out of Pancake's hands. Bennion looked at the jagged hole in the shovel. If Durwood had been a little off before because of the setting of the scope, he had adjusted his aiming now.

"It isn't worth it," Gail protested. "That gold isn't worth his killing us!"

274

"How well I know that," Pancake said somberly.

"We'll make a deal with you, Durwood!" Gail shouted, and again only silence came back.

"Durwood!" Gail yelled.

Pancake shook his head at her. "Don't waste your breath."

She steadied down, looking at Bennion, who said, "We'll make it, even if we do have to wait him out."

Pancake crawled over to Bennion. "Aren't you any good with a pistol?"

"I'll try before dark, but let's give him all the time we can afford to see if he'll come out of those rocks. He might, since he doesn't know we've got a gun."

"He knows," Pancake said. "He bumped against me coming through the rocks. I wasn't sure, but now I am. He felt the gun, Johnny. That's the reason he's forted up. Otherwise he would've sauntered over here ten minutes ago and cleaned us up like fish in a barrel."

"Then we've got a standoff."

"That isn't good enough."

All three of them knew that.

NINETEEN

The waiting was no good. They were cramped in the icy hole and the cold was sinking into them. Pancake exchanged positions with Gail. He used the shovel handle in an effort to work a peekhole between the spalls of ice, while Bennion tried to divert Durwood's attention by taking quick looks above the other end of the hole.

Durwood waited.

Pancake had almost succeeded in his task when Durwood sent a bullet crashing into the spalls. Pancake reeled back with his forehead cut from a whizzing ice fragment. He sat down and found a cigar inside his coat.

Pancake slumped there smoking, frowning into space.

The hell of the whole mess was having Gail trapped in it. Gail was all right. Pancake realized that he could be straining a little, but there was a resemblance between her and Genevieve, Pancake's long-dead sister. There should be, because Genevieve had been Gail's grandmother.

Good bloodlines; there was no doubt about it.

He looked at the two young people huddled against the wall of ice at the other end of the hole. They were looking at him as if he had lost his mind because he was taking things so easy.

They probably thought he was so old he didn't give a damn about dying.

And that was about as far from the truth as they could get. He had the years but that didn't mean he was ready to go. It didn't look good, though. By Ned, this was about as tight a fix as he'd ever got in; and because he'd let Durwood outsmart him at his own game, Johnny and Gail were caught too.

He'd meant them no harm, not Johnny and Gail, although he'd done his best to throw them clear off the track and get the bars himself. Then when he saw that was not going to work, he'd been willing to go along on a split, even with Durwood counted in.

Durwood—there was one for the book. There was a prime sonofabitch without conscience, scruples, moral values or any other real human characteristic. If he got to them with that rifle, he'd skid them down the ice like logs and dump the three of them into one of the crevasses among the *séracs*.

Bennion got up to take a quick look toward Durwood. He sat down again and stared hard at Pancake. "Who's under that headstone at Lido?"

He was guessing, Pancake knew, but he'd been guessing closer all the time. Pancake knew he'd made a good many slips; a man who talked as much as he did always piled up little errors that someone could finally put together.

Yet, Bennion was guessing. Pancake grinned and let him stew a little longer before speaking. "It's a fisherman who drowned when his boat upset. Right then, it was convenient, even urgent, for me to disappear. That fisherman had a fine funeral and his family bought a farm with the bonus I gave."

"You? Shores! Peyton R. Shores?" Gail said.

"For eighty-two years. You're Mary's girl. Her mother was my sister, your grandmother."

"I don't believe you!" Gail said.

"That's a family characteristic, for sure. Did Mary ever tell you about the Christmas in Santa Rosa when her Uncle Peyton brought her the china doll that Whoof, her terrier, tore up and broke a day later?"

Gail did not answer; she could only stare at Pancake.

"I'll tell you more when there's time. At the moment we'd better devote our conversation mainly to figuring how to get out of this little mess."

Bennion had a fast look across the spall pile. "What happened on Hellsgrin Trail?"

Pancake sighed. "You won't be worth a dime until you know, will you? All right. I was looting the Yankee. Jackson suspicioned it, but he didn't talk. My saintly brother, Victor, wasn't talking either. That Victor! He about had me nailed to the mast.

"He would have, too, if I hadn't got word that he was making a sneak visit two months earlier than he generally came. He had me, Victor did, for the difference between fifty-four and ninety-three thousand dollars. I sent Lonnie Pike to get Whingding. Lonnie was so honest it hurt, and that's why he never questioned me, until later.

"We cleaned out the mill strong room. I told him I had word that the place was going to be robbed. I took him along because he was one man who could get over Hellsgrin Trail, summer or winter." Pancake's cigar had gone out. He paused to light it.

"And you killed him," Bennion said.

"Not directly. We crossed that snowbridge, Johnny. We were above it when Lonnie got to thinking that there was something haywire. I made the mistake of offering him a bribe, and that wrecked the whole thing.

"He turned Whingding around and started back. If I had been the kind to kill in cold blood, that's when I would have done it, but I didn't. I ran along behind that burro begging and pleading with Lonnie. The snowbridge caved in when he and Whingding were crossing it on the way back."

Pancake looked straight into Bennion's eyes, and for once, Bennion was sure that he was telling the truth.

"I can hear the wind blowing yet," Pancake

said, "and the thump of that snow. There was never a sound came up from the bergschrund after the snow quit sliding. I stayed there ten minutes or more, and then I wallowed, through the drift on the trail and went back to town. I never went in the house. Alice would have known something was wrong.

"I went to Grace Bond's place and got in a monte game and stayed there until after midnight, and everyone was so drunk when I got there that they never remembered when I came, not that anyone even questioned it. I had my out. Pike was dead. I laid on him not only the fifty-four thousand, but the rest of the gold that I had spent on women and gambling in Denver and other places since the fall before."

Pancake raised up and dropped back after a flashing look across the top of the spalls. "He hasn't moved. At least the rifle still shows. I've got an idea that—"

"What about Dealer Dan?" Bennion asked. "That *is* him down there, isn't it?"

"I killed him, the only man I ever did kill. Today you'd call it temporary insanity. It was over a woman." Pancake paused. "She was worth it. He used to go down to the stable where he kept two blooded horses. He'd slip a pair of overalls over his fancy clothes and fiddle around doing such things as putting oil on the horses' hooves.

"That's what he was doing the night I went

there to talk to him. We got to arguing and he had the upper hand, making me madder all the time. I remember him straightening up from dabbing at a hoof. He put the bottle of oil he'd been using in his pocket and gave me an insulting, sneering smile and asked me what I'd pay him to leave the woman alone.

"That's when I put a pitchfork through his heart. I was so rattled I ran out of the place and clear across the creek in one of the worst snowstorms we ever had. I didn't know what I was doing. Then I got my senses back and went over to the stable again. I washed the pitchfork in the snow and threw some fresh straw around and then I dragged Dealer Dan over to that trench."

Pancake blew smoke at the sky, a sky that was warm and clear and beautifully blue high up there above the dark rocks and the cold stillness of the ice gorge. "I'm not sure that I ever felt too bad about Dealer Dan. He was a dirty bastard with women."

Pancake had planted the burro too; there was so little doubt about it that Bennion did not bother to ask.

"I've got an idea," Pancake said, "if we can figure some way to make it reach him." He began to pull misshapen sticks of dynamite from under his coat.

"How many of those have you got?" Bennion asked.

"Six. High percentage too."

"Caps and fuse?"

"I wouldn't be carrying the stuff without the fixings, would I?"

Bennion had a flash glance over the spalls.

The throw was too far for the awkward position a man would have to use from the hole, and it was likely too far for a man throwing something as light as a stick of dynamite, even if he had his feet firmly planted and room to use his arm to the fullest extent.

When Bennion sat down, the stitches Pancake had put in his wound hurt like the devil; they must have been hurting before, but he had not been aware of it. "If we can decoy him down on the ice, we can blow him right back up the hill."

"That's a terrible thing!" Gail said.

"Yep, it is," Pancake agreed, and then he clamped a cap to a fuse end with his teeth. He cut a stick of dynamite part way in two and bent the ends together. He set his knife against the fuse. "Shall we give it two inches?"

That was about ten seconds, Bennion thought. "How old is the fuse?"

"I've no idea. An inch and a half? We don't want to give him time to pick it up and toss it back."

"Would he do that?" Gail said. "I mean, could he?"

"Could and would, with a smile," Pancake said.

He cut the fuse about an inch and a half long. He gouged a hole with his knife in the soft end of one of the half sticks and seated the cap. "Now I've got to have something to wrap this package in. We don't want the cap to bounce out when it hits."

Gail began to tear up her shirt.

Bennion hefted the completed charge. The fuse was so short it seemed to have *whiff-boom!* printed all over it. He tried to estimate the reaction time between the first sputter and his windup to throw. If they did not get Durwood on the first try, he would retire out of range and the game would be over.

Pancake was making another bomb.

Bennion tore a piece from his own shirt and used it to enclose ice fragments around the package he held. That was better; the bomb had more weight, but the chances were still poor to make an accurate heave, throwing blind from the hole and from an awkward position.

He said, "We'll have to get him out in the open. Suppose we tell him we're giving up and then toss the gun toward him. Will he come down after it?"

"No," Pancake said, "but if you want to try it, empty the pistol at him before you throw it out."

That was what Bennion had in mind, but Gail objected. "It'll be more effective if you don't shoot at him."

"All right," Bennion said, "we'll give him the loaded pistol." Trying quick shots over the spall pile with a stubby pistol was an almost worthless gesture anyway. "Have you got your bomb ready, Pancake?"

"Just a minute."

Once more Bennion put his T-shirt over his head, this time cutting eyeholes so the darkness of his face would not show. Carefully he laid the dynamite charge on the edge of the hole and held a match ready to strike as he raised up. "Durwood! We're giving up. Here comes our gun!"

Gail tossed the pistol. Bennion saw it strike the ice and slide and stop about twenty feet from the edge of the glacier. "There's the pistol, Durwood!" An instant later he thought, *That would have been a fine thing to have tied a charge to for throwing.*

He saw the rifle, unmoving. Durwood gave no answer.

"What's he doing, damn him!" Pancake said.

"Nothing."

They waited and their waiting was Durwood's answer. Bennion felt his fingers holding the match growing stiff from cold and tension. Maybe Durwood would come out. Maybe he would, after he tried to figure all the angles.

At least, the T-shirt mask was working. Apparently Durwood did not see Bennion. The rifle was motionless.

After a long time Pancake settled back in the hole with a defeated grunt. Bennion kept waiting, and then he too decided they had given away much—and lost. He eased back into the hole and draped his shirt over his shoulders, realizing how cold he was beginning to feel.

His eyes met Gail's in a moment stripped of pretense and lightness. It seemed that they had known each other a long time and now they looked at each other with thoughts in their expressions that they had never brought to words. The best Bennion could do now was to smile, and Gail smiled back at him, for the moment unafraid.

Pancake said, "If he won't come out, we'll just have to figure a way to drop a present right into his nest."

Neither Gail nor Bennion heard him.

A few moments later they all heard Durwood laugh. They looked at each other narrowly, disturbed by the sound and worried. It was not a triumphant laugh, nor mocking, nor jeering, and there was no madness in the sound either, but only the pleasantness of a man who suddenly sees or hears something that he considers quite funny.

Durwood fired the rifle, three unhurried shots, but they heard no bullet action close to the hole.

"He's shooting at the pistol," Pancake said.

Bennion put the T-shirt over his head again

and had a look. The pistol was still lying where he last had seen it. Durwood's rifle barrel was angled up the glacier. It recoiled from another blast as Bennion watched.

Even before the gush of icy water rose around his feet a few moments later, Bennion knew. It was so simple and obvious that the only wonder was why Durwood had not thought of it before. Perhaps he had, but had been waiting until they threw away the pistol.

Those shots had broken the tiny dam and now the water was running again down the low place on the ice, directly into the hole. The first gush from the little pond behind the dam brought the water well above Bennion's ankles, and then it came gurgling down in a lesser stream, not much, but steady and inexhaustible.

TWENTY

Standing in the lowest part of the hole, Bennion felt the water at his knees. It was worse where Pancake and Gail were because they had to crouch or sit down. Bennion balanced the bomb in his right hand. He had to make it reach.

Then the idea came. "Give me your boot laces, Pancake!"

He did not have to tell the old man to hurry.

Bennion let the string extend about a foot from the charge, and then he tied his knife to the end of the rawhide lace so that he could grip it securely between his fingers.

Pancake needed no instruction; he was putting a throwing handle on his bomb too, and then for good measure, he added two more sticks of dynamite to the package.

"Give me another stick," Bennion said, "and then make another bomb to hold in reserve."

The water struck his beltline as he knelt on one knee in the hole, spinning the package on the end of its thong. There was room to get the leverage and room to throw, but it would still have to be a blind heave.

Even with the numbing water creeping higher, this last desperate defense could not be hurried. Bennion knew he needed at least one ranging shot. He laid the bomb up on the ice and began to make a dummy.

He ripped his shirt and wrapped it around approximately the same weight of ice as the two sticks of dynamite. He tied the package securely with part of the bootlace, and then he strapped his belt tightly around the dummy, securing it so that it would not slip. To make sure that the flapping end of the belt would not wrap around his wrist and foul the try, he cut it to the same length as the rawhide on the bomb.

"You'll have to spot the trial shot," he said to Gail, and tossed her his T-shirt.

She got thoroughly wet as she crept toward him. She slipped the T-shirt over her head and raised up cautiously.

"Ready?" Bennion said.

"Just a minute. Oh, yes, I see the rifle now."

Bennion spun the dummy, remembering that he must not lurch up when he let it go. He released it with a hard upswing, sighting the direction of its going by a high point on the spall pile.

"How's it headed?"

"It's—it's—it's clear up there, but it's off to the left."

"How far?"

"About the length of two cars."

Pancake had taken a quick look. "We'll both try. Fire up, and when I say go, light the fuse and heave away."

Bennion ripped five or six matches from a folder and struck them in one mass.

"Ready?" Pancake said.

"Ready."

"Go!"

It seemed to Bennion that the powder train would never catch. Smoke from burning tar rolled up in his face. He tipped the split fuse down, so that it was like the distended mouth of a tiny snake dipping into flame. The fuse caught, gushing quick fire.

One, two, three times around he swung the package and let it fly. He looked at Pancake. The old man was on both knees in the water at the high end of the hole. The fuse caught fire just as Bennion turned to look. Pancake whirled the package and let it go.

It was a high throw, far too high to carry to the rocks.

Only Gail saw everything that happened.

Bennion's throw was a good one. It appeared that it would carry all the way up to Durwood. Durwood must have thought so too, and he must have seen the tiny trail of white smoke. He left his hiding place and ran downhill in great leaps.

He was in the clear when Bennion's charge exploded with a shocking roar that caused ice chips to slide from the pile in front of Gail. The concussion made Durwood duck, but the force of the explosion was behind the rocks where he had been.

Neither he nor Gail saw Pancake's charge coming down from its lazy flight. Durwood stopped and fired toward the hole an instant before the second bomb exploded in the air somewhere close ahead of him.

Gail saw him fly back like a scrap of paper caught by a violent gust of wind, the rifle falling from his hands. A cloud of dirty smoke obscured her vision. "He's dead!" she cried.

Bennion fell twice getting out of the hole and over the spall pile. He grabbed up the pistol when he came to it. Durwood was sitting in the rocks, with blood at the corners of his lips and a tiny trickle of it running from his nose. His eyes were vacant as he stared at Bennion, and his mouth worked slowly, without sound.

Bennion picked up the rifle. "Where are you hurt?"

Durwood looked at him stupidly, as if he did not hear, or could not understand.

"Johnny! Come here!" Gail called.

Bennion went back across the ice. Pancake was out of the hole but he was having trouble rising. He was on his knees, waving Gail away with one hand while he tried to push himself up with the other. "I'm all right. It's just that my legs are half frozen. Give me a minute."

"You're sure you're all right?" Bennion asked.

Pancake pushed himself up until he had one foot under him and then he got to his feet with a lurch. He looked toward Durwood. "What did we do to him?"

"I don't know," Bennion said. "He's badly shocked."

"Good!" Pancake said. "I'm heading for a hot stove. You'd better pick up your lousy gold before you leave." He walked off the ice carefully.

Durwood was on his feet when Bennion went back to him, but he could not speak, and it was obvious that he could not hear either. He moved about slowly, feeling his head with both hands, or rubbing the inside of his left arm. Aside from the blood at his mouth and nose, there were no marks on him.

Gail and Bennion picked up the bars, putting them into two packs. "Can you handle it?" Bennion asked.

Gail nodded. She glanced at Durwood, wandering aimlessly along the edge of the glacier, and then she looked at the hole. It was almost full of water. Before long it would be running over, and on down to the smaller hole in the ice below. Bennion rebuilt the dam.

They had to make signals to Durwood and tug at his arm to get him started, and after that he went along with them automatically, unprotesting, unknowing.

They found Pancake on the outfall below the glacier, his back to a rock, both feet braced against the ground. He was looking down at Basin City with a strangely quiet expression in his eyes. He did not turn his head when he heard them coming.

That was when Bennion saw the blood on the left side of his jacket and on down on his hip. Bennion dropped his pack and tried to make the old man lie down.

"No! Hell no. I'm just a little shook up, that's all. I had to raise up and take a look when we heaved the dynamite. That last shot of his—it wasn't even a good one. It glanced off the ice pile and barely caught me in the side."

Pancake pushed away from the rock and went on down the trail. The only help he allowed was when they reached the head of the street, and from there Bennion held him up until they got him into a bunk in the Nose Paint.

Durwood came along like a dog that had no place to go and was grateful to be permitted in their company. They put him in a bunk also, and he lay there staring at the wall.

"You'd better tie him up," Pancake said.

Bennion turned Durwood's head and looked at his eyes, and that was more disturbing than seeing how gray and weak Pancake was. Two tiny sticks of an explosive that was scoffed at in the present day of mighty power had done that to a wonderfully intelligent mind, reduced it to the level of a stunned animal.

Bennion saw a dried trickle of blood that had run from one of Durwood's ears. He covered the man warmly with blankets and turned away.

As Pancake said, it did not seem like much, that wound in his side. When it was dressed and he was wrapped in blankets and the room was warm, he said he was all right. He drank hot coffee and called for more, and then he had to have a cigar.

Everything about Basin City seemed to have been swept from his mind. He would not talk about the glacier or about anything that had happened in the town, but he did insist on telling Gail intimate facts about her mother's family, until there was no doubt that he actually was P. R. Shores.

He dozed and then roused all through the night, and each time he was awake he had more to say to Gail.

Durwood scarcely stirred. At one time Bennion thought he was dead, but when he touched his cheek Durwood opened his eyes and said, "My head feels funny."

It was a long night. Toward morning Pancake roused from his fitful sleeping and said, "I want these whiskers shaved off, by God! I've always hated them."

They cut his beard with scissors and then Bennion shaved him. Pancake lay back with a smile, rubbing his hand over the smoothness of his cheeks. "How do I look, Gail?"

"Handsome."

"I always was, come to think of it."

Another time Pancake said, "That penny-pinching Victor, I never could stand him." He chuckled. "I had a better funeral over there in Lido than he did, even if it wasn't my own. Get me another cigar, Johnny."

Sometime around four o'clock he died. There was a faint smile on his lips, and his face still held some of the handsomeness that he had been so proud of, and he looked like a man who had taken his final leave without regretting anything.

Bennion was not surprised to see Gail cry, and this time he remembered some of Pancake's advice and tried to comfort her. In the corner by the stove Saber lay with his head between his paws and with a sadness in his look as deep as a dog can show.

By daylight Durwood had recovered some of his senses. He could talk, halting and stumbling, but he could not remember where he was or why he was here; and again it was a vacancy in his eyes that told Bennion he was not faking.

They talked about trying to walk out with him, and Bennion said, "I think we'd better wait a day. Someone is almost sure to come on over from the plane."

He was right. About eight o'clock they saw

two riders on the trail below the glacier, and when Bennion looked at them with glasses, he recognized them both, a man from the ranch next to his own, and the sheriff of Ibold County.

"Do you know them?" Gail asked.

Bennion nodded. "The one on the claybank is the sheriff. I'm happy to see him back from his vacation." He took another look with the glasses. "Do you suppose Durwood really did leave a note at the plane, saying he was here?"

"Of course not. I'll bet his message said he'd gone toward Randall. The rest of the search party is probably looking for him in that direction now."

"I think you're right."

"We'll go out with them?" Gail asked.

"We can, or we can stay and rest and start tomorrow."

"I'll take tomorrow."

"We'll have to come back," Bennion said. "At least I will. I can get someone to drive your jeep out, if you wish."

"I'll come back with you myself."

They stood side by side in the sunshine and watched the riders coming down the mountain.

Center Point Large Print
600 Brooks Road / PO Box 1
Thorndike, ME 04986-0001 USA

(207) 568-3717

US & Canada:
1 800 929-9108
www.centerpointlargeprint.com